Winter
Solstice

JoJo ,

Cherish Your Journey!

Crandall

Also by Candace Meredith

Contemplation

Losing You

www.ctupublishinggroup.com

www.amazon.com

Winter Solstice

Candace Meredith

Creative Talents Unleashed

www.ctupublishinggroup.com

CTU Publishing Group

a division of Creative Talents Unleashed

Po Box 605 Helendale, Ca 92342

www.ctupublishinggroup.com

www.creativetalentsunleashed.com

info@ctupublishinggroup.com

1st Edition

Library of Congress Control Number: 2018958574

ISBN: 978-1945791611

Book Introduction: Candace Meredith
Cover Design: Raja Williams
Editor: Shelley Mascia

Prologue

She was born on the eve of the Winter Solstice. Her first day of life was the shortest day and the longest night. Upon her birth, her mother noted a birthmark on her wrist; the pale flesh bore two overlapping crescents with a staff running down the center splitting them into two equal sides. Her first evening alone in her crib a shadow of a large man cast over her peering into her face only inches away as her mother opened the door feeling the temperature in the room drop to cold; the mere shadow of a man-like silhouette retreated through the window, his hands at his side – he was only torso and arms – his body disappeared into a stream-like fog. As her mother leaned over the rail she saw that her infant's eyes were charcoal black – her pupils dilated so that no deep brown color remained in them. Suddenly her baby burst forth in a golden fire; from slits in her back the wings of a golden Phoenix grew six feet on each side. Her infant grew into a full grown woman with long locks of auburn hair; she stood six feet tall emanating in ethereal light – the outside shimmering in a prism of thousands of shades – colors unseen by her before; on the inside she appeared hollow of the deepest, darkest black as if the depths of her span the bottomless pit of an expansive ocean. She opened her arms to her mother and began to speak: *I am Helga, Queen overseer of the light and Goddess of Celestial Light. In this body I am no longer your daughter but mother to all. It is your duty as you have been chosen to care for the infant that bares the mark of protection. And I am the Prince of Peace* an inner voice says – *Helga's inner soul and the representation of her fears, her deepest desires and her sorrow, jealousy, obsession and anger. Together we represent the dualism that is the human personality gained through experience and the human condition.*

Then the face of a man morphed into view; he had a gaunt face with high cheek bones, pointed at the chin with hazy gray eyes and thickly, arched brows who spoke: *I am master of the dark night,* he said, and retreated from view as another face morphed into view who had an attractive human face – the face of the Prince of Peace.

With those words Helga retreated back to infancy with her mother standing over her – her hand upon her chest, gasping slightly. The child she calls Alysiah Elizabeth Harp lays on her back in the crib – a smile upon her newborn's face and her deep brown eyes looking radiant with a glint of light peering in her pupil; as the light diminishes her smile fades and she begins to cry, and her mother's duty has begun.

Contents

One

On the second day, her mother Hanna anointed her skin with lavender and chamomile oils to ward off the evil that exists. She first cleansed the oils over candlelight from any impurities that may harm her daughter knowing that the ancient souls reside within her; the dualism of masculine and feminine and good versus evil is signified by the mark upon her wrist. She then blessed the ointments with an enchanted mantra she hummed like a lullaby. The enchantment *om-mani-padmi-om* pleased the ancients within; Hanna saw the spark of fire from the Phoenix twinkle in her daughter's eye. She then rubbed a vanishing cream onto her mark to disguise Alysiah's eternal nature and dressed her in a soft pink gown wrapped in a white satin blanket; she rocked her to sleep humming to her once again as her daughter's eyes went shut, Hanna could feel the warmth of her body growing stronger, warmer and brighter.

Emanating around them is a soft white light that spirals above, swirling in a clockwise pattern – guests in her house paying them a visit; they can sense and feel the presence of an eternal soul confined in the birth of the child. The white light represents the ever-after as being present in the physical realm. Her mother places a bonnet upon her head and cradles her daughter closely, basking in the warmth of radiant energy – nearing the beginning of the new century when the veil between the two worlds is at its thinnest and when evocation of the souls can take precedence – inviting them in – the protectors of the baby with the ancient soul.

"You are my daughter," her mother says, gazing into the face of a sleeping baby, "I will call you Aly my dear sweet daughter," and with that the day turns to night and the turn of the century takes place with the noise of the New Year outside her window in the brick home they share in the quaint downtown district of New Town.

On the first day of the New Year, her mother is startled by a knock on the door as the white omnipresent light recedes from the room her mother feels the sterile vacancy of the absence of radiant energy and opens the front door.

You're late on your rent again Mrs. Harp,"

the man with the robust stomach says with a pair of suspenders holding up his blue jeans.

"I know Mr. Mueller," she says, stepping out onto the front stoop, "I'll have it for you this week."

"You have four days," he says pointedly, "and if not you're out of here," he spats assuredly as he turns to walk away.

"Thank you Mr. Mueller," Hanna says faintly, closing the door.

As she does, she casually sees dark energy in the form of a damp, cold shadow wisp away down the alley following behind her landlord as she locks the deadbolt, securing them both safely inside. Hanna retreats from the foyer to the upstairs loft into her daughter's bedroom finding her newborn baby awake in the safety of her bassinet.

On this morning Hanna decides to take a long walk aside a jetted stream, on an unusually warmer day, allowing the sound of the water cascading over frozen rocks to free her mind; she needs time to think and time to make plans with Aly's best interest in mind. She places her baby into the stroller and makes her way onto the gravel laden trail that spans two miles around uninhibited wilderness, not feeling unsafe as she uses her keen awareness and intuition to know or sense the presence of danger. Hanna knows they are safe there and now she feels she can think freely; she uses her hands to sense her surroundings – lightly touching the naked honeysuckle bush, observing that only the prey have been by this way – her primary senses indicate that a squirrel moved to an adjacent tree as she looks up to find her resting in the tree.

Hanna takes a seat at a bench marked as being donated by *The Sister's Coven* – a group of women who study the ancient practices of evocation where Hanna learned meditation and the art of summoning spirits who will guide one on their journey through a mortal life. She begins to hum the mantra, this time in the expanse of the outdoors, feeling the wind gain speed, as she chants *omi-padmi-omi-om* and inhales deeply as a flock of birds soar overhead – Hanna feels the presence of divine spirits casting radiant light over both their bodies and she asks out loud for guidance: *guardians of the four corners, I ask that you grant me wisdom to help me on this journey so that we need not become homeless.* Hanna inhales deeply, feeling her spirits lifting her from within – her mind is now clear and open – she senses the awareness to know when spirit is communicating with her – to know when she senses the answer from a presence that is higher than herself.

On the walk thereafter the landscape appears serene with the beauty of nature all around her – Aly lays still as the sun, basking in its light, the mark upon her wrist begins to glow subtly, her mother sensing that its energy can only be seen by the purest, most earnest heart; she stops where she is and places her hand upon her daughter's and silently thanks spirit for the greatest gift – the life she has been chosen to protect.

With that profound knowledge Hanna leaves the serenity of nature and heads into town passing by the shops and cafes back toward her small, brick building that is nestled in the quaint town comprised of storefronts and row-homes – she parks herself on the front stoop, going within to find the answers without – on the small window pane of a blue painted door: *help needed*. Hanna believes she has been delivered her answer – from the front stoop of her own balcony.

Hanna opens the door to the shop *High Tide as a Ripple in a Pond* and finds within literature on enchantments, crystal and orbs, oils and anointments – spells on healing and cultivating divination; at the back of the store a woman hovers over the counter placing books on a shelf when she turns to find Hanna cradling her baby upon her chest.

"Hello," Hanna says, her smile gleaming, "I'm here for an application," she says, waiting patiently.

"Well I have one of those right here," the woman says, taking a step off the ladder she uses to reach the shelf; she flows elegantly in her satin dress with long curls of blond hair tucked away neatly by a burette, "here you go," she says removing paper from the cabinet beneath a register, "just fill it out and bring it on back," she says with a wide smile.

"Thank you," Hanna says, nervously and her handshakes a little.

Hanna is aged eighteen years and hasn't seen her baby's father since she told him she was pregnant –*I don't want the responsibility* she recalls him saying with a hang up followed after. Hanna was weeks into her pregnancy and felt lucky enough to have found a small one bedroom home in the cramped little town that she rents with the cash she earned waiting tables at the café; she didn't mind occupying the space in the living room to give Aly a bedroom but the money was not enough, business was slow and the owner had to let her go – and by that time she was ready to have her baby she was two weeks behind on rent.

She stood at five feet and four inches with a round belly and long, wavy jet black hair that reached her waist, with pretty hazel eyes and straight white teeth – he loved her enough before she was pregnant but took off thereafter even changing his number, wanting no more to do with her.

Hanna then worked until she was let go and paid her rent on time and did all that she could do right, then, instead of him, she found *The Sister's Coven* and learned how to chant and evoke spirit – something that made her to never feel alone again.

It was the night she walked the cobblestone street during Halloween when she met Amber, Sydney, Priscilla and Paisley. The women called themselves the Sister's Coven as they had been sworn in to protect one another against darkness. Hanna fell in love with the four women the moment she met them; Amber was the youngest at eighteen with a bobbed haircut, honey brown in color that looked glossy especially in the light. Sydney was the tallest, very elegant with curly tresses of blond hair aged twenty-two. Priscilla was the sweetest, aged twenty with dark, rich brown hair, cinnamon brown eyes and bronzed skin and Paisley, the second to the youngest, aged nineteen, had olive skin, green eyes and strawberry blond hair. The sisters tossed their arms around one another's neck when they approached Hanna; she immediately noticed their necks that were enamored with a single emerald locket, laid upon their chests from a silver necklace.

"We can help you get back at him," Amber said, stopping to remove her shoe that was rubbing at her heel.

Hanna turned to look, seeing no one else she could be talking to.

"How did you know?" She said muffled in her breath.

"We just kinda know things," Paisley said, taking a seat at a nearby bench, patting the space beside her.

"Have a seat," Sydney said, and Priscilla smiled her sweet smile.

"We use our minds to focus on the thoughts and emotions of others," Sydney said, appearing to be the leader of the group as the other three young women glanced at her often.

"It's not that I want to …"

"Not that you want to hurt him," Paisley finished her thought.

"Right." Hanna said, seated awkwardly.

"Getting back at him doesn't have to be evil," Amber said politely, "we just mean in a bad luck kind of way."

"Yeah," Paisley agreed, "like making him have an embarrassing accident."

"That's right," Sydney joined in, taking the lead, "what my sisters are trying to say is we can help him look stupid, you know, in front of others."

"But not, you know, cause him to die or anything like that," Paisley insisted.

"I understand," Hanna began…

"But you don't want to bother with him still."

"Right, I just want to…"

"Help your baby," Sydney said, taking a seat on the opposite side, tossing her arm around Hanna's shoulder.

"It's nothing to be afraid of…" Paisley mused.

"It's just that we know you were praying for your baby."

"That's right," Priscilla agreed.

"We can hear deep desires," Amber explained.

"So we came to you tonight," Sydney assured her. "We are the sisters of magic."

"Magic?"

"Of enchantments," Amber said shyly.

"Is that like witchcraft?"

The three women laughed subtly.

"Enchantment," Sydney interjected.

"Evocation," Paisley said.

"Spells," Amber added.

"We help others who ask for the help," Sydney explained.

"And we know you want protection for you and your baby," Amber said.

"So we're here to help you," Paisley said turning her eyes to Sydney.

"We can teach you all we know to help you, to protect you, to be sure that your baby is safe from harm," Sydney explained.

With that thought resting in her mind, Hanna walked the streets aside the four sisters, and began learning incantation; she learned that their necklace, barring an emerald locket, had been anointed with a protective enchantment and cleansed of impurities then consecrated with the power of the guardian.

The Guardian is an ancient soul who has the presence of a woman, the soul of a warrior, the wings of a Phoenix and one who is shrouded in a golden hue, Hanna reads from the *Book of Enchantments* she purchased before leaving *High Tide as a Ripple in a Pond.* The owner, Sterling, gave her a "new moms" discount and was sure to tell her to always do her own research before entrusting others to practice divination on her behalf.

"You don't always know ones' motivation," Sterling explained.

Hanna is seated at her Bistro table in the area made for the tiniest of kitchens in her one bedroom brick home, eating from a fruit bowl while watching her daughter who sleeps in her chair – all the while filling out the application because she is at this time jobless. "I don't need you to be homeless baby girl," she says, wiping milk from baby Aly's chin. The only job experience Hanna has is working at the café in a serving position but with that job came the responsibility of working a cash register and she quickly notes that down using the owner as her reference; she wonders if the sisters would be a good personal reference, but at this time she leaves that space blank.

Hanna grew up having few friends and was typically seen as an outcast – preferring not to talk and usually sat at the back of the class where she met Jace during their senior year of high school; then they met again in gym class where she watched him slam a soccer ball off the gymnasium wall with one swift kick being thankful that she did not have to play as goalie. She spent most her free time in his car and he took her to walk at the parks and to swim in the lake. Leaving her after learning she was pregnant was certainly devastating and Hanna took the higher road preferring to go solo, that is, until the sisters came along because her mother, a stern woman, disapproved of her pregnancy and banished Hanna from the home at the age of seventeen. Hanna learned over a short week's span that her first love was not in love with her at all and her own mother cared more for perception than having unconditional love for her own daughter.

Am I the protector of the Guardian? She thinks as she glares at the blank spaces on her application: *why me and why my daughter?*
She pulls open *The Book of Enchantments* reading the next chapter on the spirit of the Guardian: *no one must know that I have come for I am the Guardian of the night and protector of the light; I am the soul who bares all things good and evil; a secret, ancient text bound within myself as I serve to protect all of this life – ethereal and mortal, divine and sacred – I represent the war between the two worlds and must be protected by the chosen birth mother.*

Hanna quickly folds the book, slapping the pages shut, clutching her daughter into her chest –"but I must tell the sisters," she says,

pacing the confines of a small space – "they taught me the protection spells I now know."
"How am I to do this alone?" She asks aloud. She glances once again at the empty spaces and entrusts the four sisters with her mortal life ascribing each one into her list of most personal references.

The following day Hanna turns her application over to Sterling who smiles radiantly with an air of positive light – shining in her own right as best as a mortal can appear divine.
"I was wondering," Hanna says, shifting her daughter in her arms, "what you know about the Guardian?"
"The Guardian?" Sterling says, taking the application from her free hand, "there is only one and she is as enigmatic as all the great forces combined."
"What great forces?"
"The Earth, the Air, Fire and Water. And the Light."
"What is Light?"
"Radiant energy is a prism really, unlike the sun that emanates light from without, radiant light emanates from within."
"Is radiant light man or woman?"
"Radiant Light is typically thought to be feminine but one who embodies a masculine presence from within."

"Is she or he a deity?"

"The Guardian must be a discarnate who oversees the metaphysical realm."

"What do you mean by a discarnate?"

"One who does not reside within a physical body. An incarnate has a physical self-whereas a discarnate is pure energy. Pure light."

"What happens if the Guardian takes on a physical appearance?"

"That being the case," Sterling says matter-of-factly, placing her hand upon *The Book of Enchantments,* "then the two worlds are preparing for war."

"Then what would happen?" She says stiffly.

"The darkness cares to preside over the Light and to have a human following. They wage war against the good and teach one another to do harm to increase the power within."

"What's the power within look like?"

"It's dark and empty. The power within must not reign supreme – it represents our greatest fears, our insecurities, sorrow and also pure hatred."

"Who is the Prince of Peace?"

"The masculine form of the divine – the son of the Goddess."

Sterling removes a book from the shelf, "Here," she says, "I see that you are truly interested, take *The League on the Book of Enchantments Vol. II,* give it a read. From this book you will learn how to purify the human predicament from within and be ever-more protected from harm."

"But why would anyone want to harm a baby?" She stops. Thinking.

"No need to worry," Sterling says, turning her open sign to closed. "You can start the job tomorrow. But for now come with me."

Hanna follows her new boss to a darkly lit room at the back of the store.

And closes the door.

Two

In the dark room, lit only by candlelight over what appears to be a shrine, is a pentagram inscribed on the concrete floor; flowers and plants decorate the room and the shrine is filled with photographs of natural landscapes. "This is the room where you can feel safe to practice," Sterling says, waving her hand over the candle until it burns brighter.

"But what exactly am I practicing?"

"The ancient Lore."

"Lore?"

"Also called witchcraft by some. Mostly non-believers."

"Are you Pagan?"

"Only by those who practice witchcraft," she winks.

"Why do you call it Lore?"

"Somewhat like folklore, believed not to be real by most persons – and for the negative stigmatism associated with the craft."

"So then I am practicing witchcraft."

"You're practicing the ancient Lore," she smiles, "not to be confusing. But to be politically correct."

She waves her hands over Hanna's petite face; her palms glow brightly with radiant energy as she begins to chant…

The room turns to dark as the bell clangs against the glass to the front entrance.

"I know I locked the door," Sterling says, "wait right here," she says, and exits the back room.

Making her way to the front of the store she tip toes, feeling her way through the dark, stopping at the touch of a hand on her back; she turns abruptly.

"Always the wise one," Sterling says, reaching for a light switch when she hears the snap of fingers and the lights flare.

"My dear sweet sister," the woman exclaims, who stands around six feet in height with large proportions and a pointed chin with sharp jaw lines.

"You have always been adept with telekinesis," Sterling insists, "but I appreciate a knock over barging in…"

"Tisk. Tisk." Her sister says, whisking her body forward, lurking over the enchantments.

"What are you doing here, dear sister?" Sterling asks quizzically, suspicious.

"Well you know, don't you, dear little sister, I mean you are the psychic twin aren't you?"

"Born only a minute apart, I assure you don't have to emphasize smallness…"

"Oh come off it, sister," she exhales with a wry grin, "I have always been the bigger sister."

"But you have yet to say why you have come here…"

"Quite frankly," she begins, turning over a book on essential oils with the flip of a long, pointed finger, "I want to know of your recent recruits…"

"And what are you talking about?" Sterling says, fixing the book of oils on her shelf as her sister wades through the store, rattling necklaces beset with charms and power crystals.

"You do have a new recruit don't you, sister?"

"Certainly not. I only have a store and some employees."

"Employees? Really?" Her sister gasps.

Hanna paces in the back room with her daughter tucked beneath her arms. She stops before the shrine made of lively green plants and inhales deeply at the essence of radiant light emanating from the petals. She smoothes her fingers over the blooms and sniffs lightly at their sweet fragrance. In the far corner a light dimly shines and she views in that light the face of Jace, who stands amid the four sisters pleading.

"I believe we are in the presence of a clairvoyant," Sterling's sister hisses.

"Goldie, I assure you are mistaken because I close the store alone…"

A vision of Jace, who stands in the darkly lit tunnel, shouts with his arms flailing. The vision illuminates in a white light in the corner of the room and Hanna steps forward for a better view with Aly cradled to her chest.

"Couldn't stand your ground?" Sydney says.

"Hey look," he says, turning his neck to look back, "I don't even know who you are."

"But we know who you are," Paisley says.

"Oh, yeah?" He stops, facing the entrance to a long and dark tunnel.

"That's right," Amber says.

"We sure do," Priscilla chimes in.

"That's it," Sydney exclaims, "we all agree…"

"Look, like I said, I don't know who you are…"

"We're The Sisters Coven," Sydney explains.

"That would mean four sisters," Amber says, "to be frank."

"Is that right?" Jace says, opening his knapsack, "but to be frank…"

"Matter of fact?" Paisley snickers.

"I think he's being serious sisters," Sydney sneers.

"I'm warning you right now…"

"Warn us?" Priscilla smiles.

"If you follow me…"

"You'll what?" Amber beckons.

From his knapsack he withdraws a snare and lights the end, tossing the dynamite in their direction and runs off to the back of the tunnel.

The light from the flare illuminates and the vision disappears.

"What happened?" Hanna shouts at the empty, blank wall, and Sterling's sister turns to the sound snapping her fingers and the lights turn to dark.

"You must stop doing that, sister," Sterling says, hearing the raucous sound of her sister's cackle. At the snap of her fingers, the light illuminates the room, and Sterling turns to hear a scream from Hanna as her twin sister vanishes through the front door and Hanna runs madly from the room.

She screams, "My baby! My baby!"

Hanna enters the store and Sterling gasps at the now empty blanket cradled in her fingers. "Oh my God!" She exhales, "my baby girl is gone," she sobs, "Oh God," she says again, falling to her knees.

"Oh dear," Sterling says running to the front door, throwing the door open so hard the glass shatters.

"Sister! Sister!" She says.

White light emanates from her body as she forces a vision from her mind's eye seeing her sister glide through the air into a darkened tunnel and her vision turns to black.

"I must call on the elders," she says, returning to Hanna, "I'm afraid the war has begun!"

"All I want is my baby back!" Hanna exhales, burying her head into Sterling's chest.

"I know you do," she says, patting at her long hair, "and I will help you," she says bracing herself against the wall. "Tell me what happened back there … tell me what you saw if anything."

"A prism of white light, like a vision; I saw Jace and the sister's coven."

"What were they doing?"

"They were taunting him."

"And then what happened?"

"He lit a flare and threw it at them."

"And then what?"

"Jace just vanished."

"Anything else?"

"No."

"Tell me of anything at all…"

"The light diminished."

"You are clairvoyant."

"What exactly does that mean?"

"The ability to sense something beyond the primary five senses. It literally means clear seeing."

"And you?"

"I'm also a clairvoyant."

"What did you see?"

"My sister."

"Where?"

"Here at the store. But…"

"But what?"

"She might have only been a distraction and…"

"What else?"

"She may not have been here physically."

"Okay, I'm not following you."

"Bi-location. She may have been using telekinesis as a body double. Those adept in the esoteric arts also call the process astral projection."

"Can you explain?"

"A non-physical astral body."

"Did she take my daughter?"

"I don't think so."

"Then what was she doing here?"

"Snooping."

"For what?"

"I'm not sure that she was certain."

"Tell me how to get my daughter back."

"I no longer know what my sister is capable of…"

"Why would she be part of this?"

"She has a dark heart."

"For what reason?"

"Because she had a hard childhood. She wasn't pretty – the kids bullied her ruthlessly. You would never know that we are twins."

"Your twin?"

"Yes."

"Then the two of you are like good and evil."

"That's how our mother and father saw us too. I felt terrible for her…"

"But…"

"But I'm afraid of the monster she may have become."

"What can I do?"

"Use your senses. Think and feel earnestly to locate your mind's eye – use it to guide you, and I will do the same."

"Why is this happening?"

"Darkness is trying to reign supreme over the light."

"Is my daughter in danger?"

"No, not yet. They want something first. We have time to…"

"Time for what?"

"To get her back."

"I need you…"

"I know."

"I can't do this alone."

"Come with me," Sterling says, taking Hanna by the wrist, leading her to the back of the room, shutting the curtain behind them. The pentacle illuminates off the concrete floor; Sterling places her at the center of the five points and begins to chant – evoking the Guardians of the Four Corners.

So she begins.

Three

The Guardian of the North Tower is tall, thin, with a pointed chin, slightly crooked nose, dressed in black with equally dark hair that falls past her shoulders.

"Isn't she evil?"

"Don't be so brash to confuse style with evil, young one."

"She prefers the look of Avant Garde" Sterling explains.

"I'm the Guardian of the North Tower – quite frankly, young dear, I harmonize the balance between good and evil."

"Why would you want evil to exist?"

"Certainly," she says, turning to Sterling, "she knows of balanced energies."

"You cannot comprehend one without the other," Sterling explains.

"I see that both energies are in balance. Like a healthy anger – but nothing of cruelness."

"How did you get here? I mean from where exactly …"

"I live in the Northern hemisphere but I never say precisely where."

"The Guardians …"

"Now," she interrupts, "the question is what am I doing here?"

"My baby…"

"She has gone missing."

"My senses have alarmed me… of course you don't think that Goldie has anything to do with this?"

"Of course not," a voice says as a vortex opens within the room as the twin sister steps through the port hole.

"Certainly sister, you must not…"

"Please explain your presence here…"

"Well it's okay for one sister to visit another is it not…"

"It certainly is," Leisha, of the North Tower says.

Another port hole opens and a short, squat woman passes through; she is dressed in vintage attire – a dress made of patchwork; she appears "homely" and smiles with pearly white teeth nestled between long strands of ashy brown hair.

"Say," she says, not reducing her smile, "what gives the privilege for such company?"

"Your graces are called to aid the Coven during this vulnerable time."

"Vulnerable?" She says, unfurling her garments.

"Someone has taken my baby. My daughter."

"You don't say? Oh my, I must know more…"

"First, let me introduce you cousin," Goldie pipes in, "this is the Witch of the East, Gladys."

"That is I," she says, bubbly.

"And this is my store clerk. And friend. Hanna." Sterling explains.

"Nice to meet you dear," Gladys says, taking her stance at the Eastern port of the Pentagram. "Shall we continue evocation first then?" She says.

"Yes, cousin," Goldie says.

"We shall," Sterling says, taking her stance at the center of the pentagram aside Hanna; Leisha is at the North, Gladys at the East and Goldie stands as overseer amid the South as they summons the Guardian.

"Guardian of the South," Sterling begins, humming a dissonant mantra, "we call on you."

"Portal to the South, open," Leisha says.

"Grace us with your presence cousin," Gladys says.

And Goldie chants in a similar hum the mantra "omi-padmi-omi-om!"

"Open," they say in unison as the portal opens in a beaming vortex of immense light; a woman emerges, her hair is cut like a short bobbed style, blond, and she has crystal blue eyes; she wears a fitting red tank, a skirt past the knees and tall black boots.

"Elusha at your request sister," she says nodding to her right.

"Good to have you join us," Gladys says.

"We will explain shortly, dear cousin," Goldie says as she canters to the left of the Pentagram and they begin to evoke the remaining Guardian of the West tower.

Sterling chants, "omi-padmi-omi-om."

"We call on the Guardian of the West Tower," those in the Pentagram say in unison, "open."

The portal opens wide and bright as the vortex spirals in motion; the remaining Guardian passes through; a woman nearing forty years of age with two long braids down her back and beaming brown eyes; she bows her head, "cousins," she says, snapping her fingers, and the vortex closes.

"Vienna," Sterling says, "welcome."

"We are all united," Gladys says, and Sterling begins hugging each one.

The evening after, Hanna walks the dark tunnel where her vision last showed Jace had been. She ponders over how much the sisters had showed her – how much their knowledge would aid her in protecting her daughter; she thinks about Jace – why he abandoned them. She reaches the end of the tunnel and comes to face a statue of George Washington and breaks into a sob, then her emotions become angered and she picks up stones – tosses each one, lunging and hurling them forward; each one ricochets from his astute expression.

"Tell me where to find my daughter," she exhales, bellowing loudly onto the statue. "You're dead! You're there! In that place where they exist! Tell me who took my daughter!"

She screams, raging, hurling rocks one after another then she sees Jace; she turns abruptly as he stands aside the darkness; she picks up the stones and hurls them again – Jace's average frame moves gracefully – his athletic body dives to miss but takes one to the forehead.

"What?" He glowers, "what can I do?"

"You could leave asshole! How about that?"

"I did…" he begins to stutter. "I did the best thing that I could do," he says, wiping blood from above his eye. His sandy blond hair is stained in crimson.

"How can that possibly be the best you can do?"

"I didn't want to fuck her up."

"What are you talking about?"

"I've been trying to find you."

"Well here I am!"

"I know…"

"And your daughter," she sobs, "is gone Jace! Someone took her!"

"When?"

"Yesterday. At this time yesterday!"

"You made friends with those bitches."

"They helped me."

"They're no one you can trust."

"What do you know?"

In the coolness of the evening during a frost in January, Jace places his hand over his heart and makes the promise to find his daughter…

"Only because the sisters threatened you!"

"No. I'm a changed guy. And I'm going to help you."

Hanna places her head to his shoulder leaning in to him, pressing her lips to his ear, "You better find her," she warns him, and he takes her face into his hands, speaking deliberately, closely, "I will."

Hanna wakes after a long, restless sleep thinking that all had been a dream. But she is in her bed. No longer asleep but the image is fresh in her mind; she saw the same gaunt face in her state of half sleep. A croaky voice whispered to her: *I am here.*

"Who are you?" She had said, turning in her sleep, her heart rate accelerated, starting to panic, and her eyelids fluttered.

"I am your friend," the voice said, amidst in her half sleep.

But she recognized the face as having been the gaunt one that emanated from her daughter in the lucid vision.

"Where are you?"

"I am in your dreams."

"But where are you in my dream? Where am I?"

"I might be in your room."

"But you're not. You're in my head."

"I'm in your dream. In New England."

"Should I find you?"

And with that he vanished.

She turns to her bedside table and turns the light on. She then reaches for her phone from the table and dials for Jace.

He answers in a groggy voice.

"Meet me at the tunnel right now," she says.

"What?" He stutters.

"Don't ask. Just do it."

"Listen…"

She ends the call and pulls on her blue jeans and baggy sweatshirt heading out the door. At the tunnel he's already there, tossing his hands into the air, "Are you freaking crazy?"

"No." She says pointedly. "I'm not. I have something I must tell you."

"Here? Now?"

"Yes."

"Well, what is it?"

"Aly is special."

"I know." He stammers, running his hand through his hair. "But come on… why did you have to bring me here… to tell me…"

"That she's gifted."

"What are you talking about? Isn't she a little too young to know..."

"She possesses super natural beings."

"What?" He faintly chuckles when a rat scurries into the tunnel.

On the interior wall, Sterling appears just from the neck up, in a vision shrouded with light, "That's a totem pet," she says, carefully.

"A what?" Hanna asks, staring blankly at the wall..."

"What the hell? Who the hell are you talking to?" Jace stammers.

"Sterling. My boss. She's channeling..."

"She's what?"

"She's channeling mental energy to talk to me."

"What the fuck?"

"I'm trying to tell you..."

"I think you might need to try harder."

"What's a totem pet?" She whispers.

"In ancient Lore a totem is an animal, a spirit being, sacred to its beholder as a guide that is connected to its human... likely to be my sister's. Just be careful. Keep your instincts about you. Follow your intuition."

And with that message, she vanishes. Jace appears perplexed and annoyed at the same time.

"This must be some serious shit."

"Those four sisters, women, you met, they're Pagan, you know?"

"No, I don't know."

"They practice Witchcraft."

"Come on…"

"No, listen, Aly is special and someone has taken her…"

"I said I would help you."

"But you need to know that we're up against witches. Probably a Warlock, or Warlocks."

"Okay, I'm really lost here."

"I can see things…"

"What things?"

"Tonight. In a dream."

"But a dream is nothing but…"

"No. He. It. Spoke to me."

"What did it say?"

"He might be close. He said he's in New England."

"What? Like Vermont?"

"Possibly. Or maybe further Northeast."

"Maine?"

"I don't know."

"Why Maine?"

"I don't know."

"But what else do you know?"

"Only that someone has taken our daughter and it might be to aid a demon… one that might be in the Northeast somewhere."

"Okay," He stammers again, "but what did the wall just tell you?"

"Sterling told me there's a totem…" She whispers.

"Why are you whispering? There's no one out here."

"The totem is an animal spirit used by Wiccan people, but this one could be used by one that is evil."

"Who exactly?"

"Goldie."

"Goldie?"

"Sterling's twin."

"Tell me why she's evil," Jace says faintly.

"Literally. Because she has a troubled past."

"Can she lead us to Aly?"

"That's possible."

"Then that's where we begin."

"How?"

"We need to get in her head."

With that the rat scurries out the entrance of the tunnel, passing over the feet of the Washington statue.

"We have to be careful," Hanna says.

"I know. But for now, get to know her as a friend."

"Okay."

Together they enter the night looking at the dark sky, silently asking the stars – guide us. In the following week, Hanna packs her belongings and moves into Jace's one bedroom apartment. She sleeps on the sofa.

She cannot focus on work; not until she finds her daughter. Her nights are restless. She sobs.

The twilight hours bring out a voice at the back of her mind – New England – but why does she feel they are in Maine? Perhaps she feels there is a great distance between her and her daughter. The separation feels dramatic. She sloshes some cold water over her face, towel dries her wet face and takes a seat on the bathroom floor. She enters full meditation – reaching deep within her psyche, asking her higher self to guide her; she transcends time and space that is limited by basic consciousness and finds a small light, illuminated upon the tunnel rat; she asks the rat: where have you gone? She waits, listening, observing the plump little creature … they left Boston, he hisses with pointed teeth, and her eyes flicker open. The sun light illuminates, reflecting off the mirror.

"They're leaving Boston?" She says aloud.

Hanna moves outside onto the balcony on the second floor and asks the purple sky, "Is there a totem spirit present?" She lifts her glance to the nearby electrical pole where a bird of prey – the Red Tailed Hawk – tuffs up its wings, bobs its head and flies toward the Northeast. Unexpectedly an apparition appears behind her that morphs into plain view.

"Sydney?" Hanna says, startled.

"Sister…" She says back.

"How…?"

"You know now, sister. We witches teleport. We call it Astral Travel."

"But I thought that was typically an out-of-body experience."

"Advanced witches learn how to dematerialize – then materialize in another location at will, usually."

"Usually?"

"Nothing is perfect."

"Then you could…"

"Help you get your daughter back."

"How did you…"

"No need to ask, right?"

"Right."

"Advanced minds tune into the emotional vibrations of another – a deep form of empathy."

"Right."

"Can you see my daughter?"

"No. Unfortunately she may be in the possession of an advanced demon. Not just a Warlock. But an advanced evil."

"Why?"

"He seeks power of course. And you said it yourself … Aly is special."

"Why can't she just…"

"Be a normal child? She is. And Sterling told you about totem guides but be more vigilant – more adept witches can be a shape shifter who transforms into other people or animals. Don't let them mislead you. A totem pet acts as a guide so also be on the lookout for an observant other."

"Certainly Sterling isn't being misleading?"

"Not intentionally. One doesn't know all when it comes to The Craft."

With that message, the sun breaks over the horizon and the Hawk returns to the highest point. Cawing.

It may be time to begin following her guide.

Candace Meredith

Four

The vision of Sterling glimmers from the shower curtain.

"Come to the store," she says.

"What about Jace?" Hanna asks, wrapped in a towel, her hair still dripping – soap suds fall from her cheeks.

"Never mind him now. The Craft cannot tolerate disbelievers."

"But he says he will help," she whispers.

"No need. Don't worry. Just come soon."

Hanna tosses her towel to the floor as the vision vanishes.

She puts on heavy cargo pants lined with cotton, feeling she'll need to be warm and practical. She pulls over a hooded sweatshirt atop a thermal undershirt and ties her hair with a band, sticking a cover on her head that's marked with military badges – a find from the Salvation Army during a year in Junior High when she volunteered for Christmas.

She steps out of the bathroom into the hallway coming face-to-face with Jace.

"Where are you going?" He asks, drinking from a flask.

"It's Sterling. She's calling on a meeting."

"What kind of a meeting?"

"I'm not sure but wait for me. I'll be back."

She laces her boots, stuffs flares into her pockets she found in the closet and pulls a Gore-Tex jacket over her attire and closes the door behind her.

"I'll come with you," Jace says through the crack.

"No need," she says, "I won't be long."

She passes through the familiar tunnel by foot, never affording a car, and finds the rat scurrying past the exit, out into the frozen landscape.

Above the tree line in the night sky she finds the Red Tailed Hawk who extends its wings and dives toward the rat, forcing the creature into the nearby gutter.

"You are my guide now," Hanna says, extending her arm. "Sage," she says, "your name is Sage. Farewell my friend," and she takes flight, never too far away.

She pulls at the front door entrance that has been left unlocked and moves to the back room; there, she is astonished to find a large group of nearly twenty men who are seated in rows of pews that were hidden behind a curtain. Sterling's store is also a sanctuary. the Pentagram burns bright with luminescence. Sterling stands at the front of the open room, drinks are provided in a golden chalice and the Guardians are gathered together in the pew at the front of the room.

"Welcome," Sterling says, "please be seated."

Wasting no time, she takes her stance at the small podium.

Now we are all present I am going to begin then we shall proceed with introductions. I have called The Warlock Coven, the assembly of men you find here this evening Hanna, to explain that the Dark Army is merging to form a rally against its enemies: those who follow the light.

"How do you know this is the truth?" One of the men says.

A child has been stolen and is likely in the possession of the darkest of men; a demonic presence.

"Whose child?"

"Hanna's child."

"My daughter," she says, raising her hand.

"The child possesses a birthmark – the mark of darkness and the light."

The men sit in their silence.

This means the war is upon us; the child is the birth of the highest order in a mortal body. They were hidden from the metaphysical dimensions but they have been found here.

Goldie slits her eyes in the direction of the men who turn their eyes onto each other.

"My sister has called upon you to aid us in gathering the order of the East."

"The entire order?"

"Yes," Sterling says, "we will move toward Vermont, and continue toward the Northeast where at the highest summit the Dark Army may be presiding. Leisha, The Guardian of the North, has insight into the minds of dark forces. Mount Katahdin – the greatest of highest summits and home to the God of Storms – this is where the sky will part and from the fifth dimension it will rain a dark cloud of followers. This is written in the Ordinance of the Oracle; the prophecy of all prophecies."

"We are here to help you, sister coven," one of them says, extending his hand to Hanna.

She stands to take his hand.

"I am Luther," he says, standing tall with broad shoulders, a long graying beard and wavy hair, as the rest of the men stand, forming a line, they shake hands with Hanna.

"I am Richard," the next one says, looking proud with a defined physique.

"I am Matthew," the third says, a shorter stout man with thin lips.

"And I am Bill."

"Names Ted," The fifth says, "nice to meet you Hanna," and he takes a stance at the back of the room appearing serious with dark features.

"I'm Lucius," the young one says.

"I'm Marcus," the seventh says, and bows his head; he is tall, thin and rough on the edges.

"I'm Grant," the next says, "we are the Coven of Worcestershire Street – a Coven of over twenty members. Nineteen are present today, but the rest will be joining. We are to leave ahead of the Sister Coven and The Guardians."

"We will be leaving by foot," Sterling says, "since Hanna is not adept in Astral Travel. Our guides will lead us."

"All those birds?" Hanna asks.

"The Ravens," Leisha says.

"Yes," Hanna replies.

"They are a panoramic view of the forest," Sterling explains.

The men continue in the single file line and introduce themselves, before stepping through a portal as they dematerialize and travel the cosmos to their destination: Northward.

"I shall go as well, brothers," Goldie says, "to be of assistance during your journey."

"That would be best, sister," Sterling says.

Sterling gathers the women together around a cauldron at the front of the room. She appears within the water vapor of the steaming pot, "This is a practice known as scrying," she says to Hanna, extending her hand for her to take a stance beside her.

"The practice enables a clairvoyant to have a vehicle for foretelling the future, or in your case, to see into the mind of another. All oracles of divination can be useful tools for foresight but I find that the vapor steam also clears the mind so the translucent body can come forth enabling the conscious mind to relax. Your ability to see may enable you to find the thing that is most precious to you – your daughter."

Hanna kneels, placing her face over the cauldron as water vapor clears her mind's eye and Vienna begins chanting the meditative mantra.

The Guardians begin to hum and Sterling sings like a bell: "Peace, peace, peace," she says, to bring out a calming environment in which Hanna can work.

With the steaming cauldron engulfing her face, she begins to see with clear senses. Jace comes into view standing outside his apartment door and Goldie morphs into view; she holds her totem rat in her left palm, stroking its back with curled fingers. Jace has both hands in his pockets, trying to remain calm and casual. Goldie slits her eyes over her left shoulder but the vision remains stiff and visual. Jace carries a knapsack and shuffles his feet.

"Consider yourself warned," she says with a grin and proceeds down the stairs, glancing up one last time, peering through the banister, wrinkling her brow. Jace slams the front door and the vision recedes to a steamy cauldron.

"Goldie warned Jace," she says, muffled under her breath.

"I wonder of what?" Sterling asks.

"I don't know. I could only hear her say consider yourself warned."

"Perhaps she knows more then."

"I want to see my daughter," she sobs.

"You have a very strong group of support. We understand your pain, and we'll do all that we can."

"Thank you," Hanna says, burying her face into her hands.

"What did she see, sister?" Leisha asks, stepping toward the now cooling cauldron.

"Her vision was incomplete."

"We must try again," Hanna says.

"Yes, we must," Leisha adds.

"We will. Tomorrow is the night of a quarter moon; the energies should be well aligned." Sterling insists.

"We will help you, sister," Gladys says.

"Surely we all need to be together … Goldie must oversee …" Leisha says.

"Goldie's expertise is in Telekinesis, sister. Certainly she can help," Sterling says candidly.

"Yes. Agreed." Leisha says.

"The Sister's Coven are adept at teleporting," Hanna explains.

"You can call on them when it is time." Sterling insists.

"Then what is our first step, sister?" Vienna casually pipes in.

"To Boston." Sterling insists, "To find out what we can there."

"Then what?"

"First to New Hampshire and Vermont, then we continue Northeast."

"The Covens are strong there," Elusha says, with a comforting smile and a slight bow.

"Yes, cousin," Sterling says.

Sterling waves her hands over the candle flames and the light goes out.

The front door clangs and Goldie glides through, snapping her fingers and the lights flicker.

In the early Dawn hours, Jace steps off the balcony of his second floor apartment, places his filled pack on his back and makes his way through the tunnel. There, he finds eyes peering through the dark that approaches as he grabs for the knapsack, armed with flares and receives a sniff and a lick to his hand.

"Thor," he exhales, tossing his pack to the ground as the gray and white creature puts two paws to his chest, pushing him to the ground. The Wolfhound whines with gratitude and love. Jace runs his hand over his thickly, matted fur, "Where the hell have you been?" He bellows, picking the dog off all four paws, cradling him in his arms. Thor peers in his face with topaz eyes and gives a lick to his face. The reunion is both emotional and ecstatic – Jace finds a locket upon his thick leather collar and removes it; the locket is enamored with an emerald stone and on the inside is an amulet of a gargoyle with the sun and the moon in its clutch. Jace places the stone around his neck and wrestles Thor to the ground, a tear on his cheek, "There's a reason you're back, buddy," he says, leading his beloved pet to the apartment where he finds a white satin blanket, Aly's blanket, and he gives the blanket to Thor who sniffs violently, pawing at the remnants of oil scents – giving a long dissonant howl, and the Raven pecks at the window sill.

At the sound of the wolf howling, the rat scurries underground and there is movement erupting in the East.

Then all is silent and the sunlight breaks over the horizon.

The Sister's Coven gathers together, feeling they let her down; they huddle by candlelight to chant, not knowing why the sacred enchantments did not protect baby Alysiah from potential harm. In a circle around the flickering of light they hold hands and hum in monotone to evoke spirit. They call on the guide of incarnates; from the emerald stones a light bursts forth - an inward light emanates from within and a green-eyed cat emerges. Solid black fur glistens like silk and the creature bellows a loud roar before taking a stance at the center of the circle.

"Brother cat," Sydney beckons, "lead us to the chosen one…" and she anoints the black cat with scented oils and he purrs, licking a paw while stretching his hind legs and peers into the night sky; he gives a soft roar to the North Star. From an open ledge he jumps forth toward the moonlight and a Raven flies overhead, in the talons of a Red Tailed Hawk, squirms the rat and the Panther climbs high above sniffing the Eastward breeze.

Hanna dreams lucidly about her daughter. She is placed in a dark chamber with an old woman who has pointed fingers; she places runes over Aly's body, reading each one like a great fortune teller. Her teeth are covered like moss and her frizzy hair lays down her back. The old woman peers over the baby and bellows a hiss, waving her bony knuckles over Aly who lies sleeping.

She wakes from her bed, breathing heavy, running to the bedroom, but Jace is not there. *Tomorrow,* she thinks, *we are due to leave.*

Where are you, Jace? She approaches the nearby window waving her arm – the Hawk flies overhead, takes notice and lands on the balcony. Hanna enters the frigid air and waves a tee-shirt by her beak. The Hawk clutches the shirt in its talons and takes flight. In the dark night, Jace walks the park looking for any sign of Hanna when the Hawk drops the shirt from its talons and Thor begins to howl; the black cat takes notice and retreats. He re-enters the circle, takes a leap toward the flame, and vanishes; the sisters close their emerald lockets upon their neck, "Thank you, proud creature of the night," Sydney says.

"Nocturnal pet," Amber says.

"Our true guide," Priscilla adds.

"We honor you," says Paisley.

The Sister's Coven close the circle by taking a bow toward the center flame when Sydney blows the candle out and beyond the window there is a full moon.

Goldie snaps her fingers again and the lights begin to dance. The atmosphere is complete with the presence of the full moon. Hanna steps through the front door; the sky is abundant with Ravens cawing overhead with the Hawk upon the street light. A rat peers from its perch on the cobblestone street and a loud howl beckons in the distance.

"I have called together this committee for the night is lush with the presence of the new moon."

"What do you have in mind, sister?" Sterling asks.

"Evocation. In a séance."

Sterling gasps, "Certainly we are not ready."

"Nonsense." Leisha says, "We are the Guardians of the four corners."

"But Hanna is not ready."

"I just want my daughter back," she interjects.

"Evocation is very serious," Sterling explains.

"I can handle it. I promise."

"I'm sure she's ready, sister," Goldie insists. She enters the back room with Leisha following behind and removes a curtain from the evocation circle where she has placed a round table. She places a black orb at the center and The Guardians follow behind.

"Whatever happens," Sterling whispers, "do not be afraid of getting your daughter back."

In the corner of the room Goldie lights two sconces and The Guardians take a seat around the table. They hold hands and begin the call for evocation.

"Great Warrior of the night," Goldie begins…

"Who are we evoking?" Hanna whispers.

"We are calling on the one who has stolen her."

Goldie hums in a chant and the Ravens caw, flapping their wings violently, swarming the streets.

She hums louder in a monotonous incantation.

"Greatness of the night," she begins, "I call on you to join this coven of your own free will."

Sterling's fingers turn to cold and Hanna takes notice as her hands begin to shake.

"Stay strong," Sterling muffles beneath her breath.

In the room a great presence begins to form: the being is half beast with grisly, fanged teeth, long out-stretched arms, elongated fingers like that of a gargoyle with strands of fur down its back and feathers for a mane.

He spreads his body and breathes deeply.

"Where is my daughter?" Hanna screams forcefully.

"Just wait calmly," Sterling says, "wait to see if…"

"Hush your tongues," Goldie glowers and Leisha smiles with pointed teeth.

"Guardian of the North," Goldie continues…

"Sister," She replies.

"Aid me in the name of the master…"

"Ruler of the night," she says, bowing her head…

"You're both evil!" Hanna shouts, nervously, but with utter authority as Sterling stands form her chair, but the ancient beast grasps her in its claw-like talons and bites into her neck, deeply, forcefully, puncturing her jugular; she cannot speak and Goldie slits her eyes while Leisha stands and takes a bow.

"Sterling," Vienna and Gladys say in unison. Vienna inhales, gasping; The Guardians of the East and the West stand in unison, extending their arms to the center circle; their fingertips glimmer slightly as they focus divine light upon the beast but he hisses a large growl, biting her neck again until her lifeless body falls to the table.

"No!" Screams the Guardians.

"Help her, you monster!" Hanna bellows as Goldie removes a staff from her long, black garment and a flash like lightning strikes her body and she is sent careening through the air, suspended against the wall.

"Sisters," Gladys steps forward, "this is of the upmost evil," she begins as the air becomes stagnant and Vienna begins to cough – the heavy weight of air, like decay, suffocates her.

"You cannot be this cruel, dear sister," Elusha says, wiping away a tear.

"Don't be so pathetic," Goldie hisses, "my sister knew of her fate long before, as my master, the ruler of death and of life, must make use of her body – her blood feeds his most dire appetite."

"We shall rule at his side," Leisha says, "certainly your sister knew…"

"She made the grave decision long ago to rule against the one great master."

As the blood of the divine follower seeps from his lips he begins to speak…

"And now you are mother to the child." He spews as he speaks, with his back arched and his teeth stained in crimson.

"No!" Hanna exhales.

"Leave us!" Gladys pleads.

"I am done with you." Goldie spats as Hanna drops to the floor.

Leisha smirks, taking a bow toward her ruler and takes Goldie's hand; together, they form a trinity of evil and the lights go out.

Candace Meredith

Five

"Where have you been?" Jace exhales, out of breath, running through the tunnel. Hanna drags her feet in a daze-like state. Jace grabs her face in both hands, "Where have you been?"

"It's Sterling," she muffles.

"Look," he says, hurriedly, "I have some things to show you!"

"What," she stammers.

"It's Thor, he's back!"

She lets out a loud gasp and begins hitting him in his chest, forcefully flailing, "My baby was stolen from her blanket! And you're telling me you got your dog back?" She screams.

"There's more to it," He says, holding onto her tightly with both arms.

"What more?" She cries, falling to her knees.

"This," he says, removing a book from his knapsack. "The Book of Prophecy and Prophetic Dreams."

"Where did you get that?"

"It came in the mail."

"Sterling," she sobs, "she must have sent it. She must have known." She cries.

"I'm only coming back to collect what little I can…"

"Then what?"

"There's a movement."

"The Prophecy talks about the storm…"

"In the North?" Hanna sniffles. "The Northern Guardian … she has sided with Goldie."

"Who is she?"

"The one who warned you … Sterling's twin … and …"

"That woman," he stutters, "who chided on about those friends of yours."

"Oh? The Sister's Coven! That was her warning? But why?"

"She said that I'd be followed. And … taunted."

"That's not much of a warning."

"But how can you trust a woman who carries a rat?"

"Not even Sterling trusted her."

"We need to make a pact right now."

"Okay?"

"To get our daughter back! And Thor is more than a dog – he is part wolf and he can navigate the forests."

"Yes," she clamors, "we are her parents! We should do this!"

"We need to pack. And be prepared."

"I must attend the funeral."

"When?"

"This evening. At midnight. Her body will lay in a bed of roses and they practice the sacred ritual of burning the mortal body to release the sacred body to the afterlife."

"I want to come with you."

"I pray her soul can lead us."

"We have much to talk about. But later. We have much to do."

"Yes," she exhales a deep sigh, and they hold one another before departing.

Back at the apartment, Jace packs the essentials to be used for a treacherous hike toward the highest summit: a pick axe, portable shovel, poncho, two-man camping tent, lighter, lighter fluid, canteen, dry food, extra socks and parka, and the *Book of Prophecy*.

He gives Thor a rub on the head, "Help me find her," he says, as Thor sniffs a pile of her clothing and begins to howl.

"Shhh," Hanna says.

"Not now ,Thor," Jace agrees.

They pack extra water and head outdoors in the cool breeze. They hike by foot with a dim flashlight and enter the tunnel, feeling like the last time; the tunnel adjoins the New Town district and the wilderness where Hanna liked to take her baby for a walk if the weather allowed. She reaches the park bench marked *The Sister's Coven* and rubs her fingers over the insignia: "I need you," she whispers.

"Who?" Jace whispers back.

"My friends. And Sterling."

In the night breeze the air brings on the slightest vortex and shimmering with light the Sister's Coven appear.

"At your call, sister," Sydney says,

"We shall join you," Amber says.

"Merry to meet you, sister," Priscilla says.

"We have come to you," Paisley adds.

"The power of focus, mindfulness and attention excels in this coven," Sydney says as they place the emerald amulets in their clasped hands and hum a dissonant mantra; the dark cat emerges, and Thor sniffs at the creature as they exchange their curiosity.

The cat climbs the nearest tree and perches on its branches while Thor lies beneath the bare naked tree.

"As above. So below," Sydney says.

"Our totem guides have united," Paisley explains.

"Dogs don't like cats," Jace spats.

"Stay calm angry one," Sydney spats back.

"We were just toying with you," Amber says.

"You cost us our daughter!" He bellows.

"You cost you your daughter!" Amber hollers.

"Enough!" Sydney says, forcing herself between them, "The dark others have fooled us all – the past is done – it is time to move on."

"Yes," Hanna agrees, "but why are you helping us?"

"Your daughter bares the mark of the Goddess of War and Queen of the Light; Lord of peace, tranquility and compassion."

"The mark is written about in The Book of Prophecy," Amber says.

"Jace has the book. It was likely sent by Sterling before…"

"Before what?" Sydney says.

"Before that monster killed her."

"The death of a divine follower is most tragic," Sydney bows her head.

"She was my only hope."

"You, we, are not hopeless," Jace fumes.

"I just need to feel her again."

"And that's just what we'll do!" He yells.

"You didn't want her you creep!" Paisley screams.

"No more!" Sydney interjects.

"This isn't going to help us," Hanna says.

"No sister, and we will be even more vigilant!" Sydney agrees.

"I have a Hawk for that."

"But you also have us. And we come with the stealth of a very intelligent guide."

"Keen senses," Amber adds.

"But Sterling thought I had that as well…"

"You could not see what was hidden."

"No. She was right in front of our faces."

"That's where Sterling wanted her to be."

"You keep your friends close but your enemies closer," Jace adds.

"But why? It solved nothing."

"You first had to know your enemy."

"Now we know her strengths," Jace says.

"Her weaknesses," Amber admits.

"How?"

"Attaching her to your mind," Sydney suggests.

"Brains are private places."

"Minds not so much."

As the sun recedes in the West, the mountain is illuminated by a backdrop of pink and fuchsia hues.

Hanna carries the torch to an unmarked site and the three Covens unite: The Guardians, the Four Sisters and The Warlocks.

The Guardians washed and anointed her body with oils, and dressed her body with white robes; Vienna brushed her long locks of blond hair and then she was placed on a high bed. At the time of *Prothesis* the Covens gathered to pay respect to their beloved sister and the *Ekphora* presided near dawn; very minimal objects were placed in the grave but a lone Raven cawed above and the Guardians stood weeping.

Hanna sobs and shakes while Jace puts his free arm around her and in the other hand is

Sage – sitting gracefully with a lowered upper body – a totem's respect. The torch is held high at the break of dawn after five hours of mourning and as the high bed of debris ignites, her soul departs from high above as the bare naked trees sway in the breeze and the sky turns to purple.

The men form an assembly line, each places one branch into the flames, and mark her grave with a staff made of marble – the mourners pay respect and use divination in the presence of the soul of an elite witch who was adept in ancient lore; the twigs, anointed with oil, show in hues of lilac and jade and the scent of lavender permeates the landscape as the Raven flies high above them.

In the twilight hours of the following day, Hanna places her hand upon the marble orb at the end of the long staff and inhales deeply; she feels for her presence and peers into the cosmos when she hears her voice: *never be alone,* her voice says. Hanna looks over her shoulder to see footprints in the earth where no one has stood; then the grizzly sound of a harrowing growl turns to her – a spirit presence unseen by her naked eye startles the Raven that swoops from above and the beast yelps; it carries the sound of the hissing beast she saw in Sterling's store – and she thinks it is time to gather there once more.

In their meeting, the Warlock's Coven ascribe an insignia of a High Priestess upon the totem pole; the Raven is whittled into wood with eyes that are steady peering through darkness. The totem pole, erected at Sterling's grave, is marked to serve as a reminder of her devotion to contemporary (and ancient) practices of Paganism.

Together they form a circle with their arms stretched as if they are transcending the cosmos and they chant in harmony to bring peace to the hearts of evil men and women.

"I miss the light you radiate," Hanna says as she places her palm to the marble orb and points her face to the Raven – "I ask to be your mother now," she says, and lifts her arm to the wind as the Raven flutters to the ground beside the totem cawing, "come with me," she says, and the Raven moves to her open hand tilting its face to the sun.

At the break of the following day, the movement to Boston coincidentally takes them to the festival for Pagan Pride Day; there they hope to locate powerful covens – those who will be prepared for the Day of Storms.

The streets of Boston roars with Pagans; the community is live with Wiccan rituals and practices. Healing and divination is being taught among Sacred Circles, Tarot cards and Runes are being used in foresight practices, and a discussion on consecration of Wiccan tools: incense, bells, water, pentacle, chalice, candles, cauldron and an altar to pay respect to the Gods and the Goddesses is centered in the circle.

There is a gathering of over four hundred Witches and Warlocks; the Warlock's Coven pays respect to the Goddess of War at the foot of the altar that is decorated for the dark season. Jace opens the *Book of Prophecy* and points to the article on the Goddess of Storms and the coming of the dark war; a war that is to follow the birth of the Goddess who inhabits a mortal body.

"The dark followers wish to possess the followers of the light and sway them into evil and empowerment of the self," Jace says.
"Couldn't the Goddess of Storms be Goldie herself?" Hanna says, exasperated with her revelation.
"And the Guardian of the North…"
"Leisha," Hanna says.
"They are overseers of storms of the North."

"The Reason the Prophecy marks the War in the far North."

"The highest summit."

"They are to lead us there…"

"It's inevitable, Hanna."

"Why? Why can't we stop them?"

"That's precisely what we're aiming to do. But the war is inevitable."

"Now do you believe in magic?"

"No. I believe that people, like them, are capable of evil. Those bitches are starved for power."

"Power at any cost."

"Even the death of a sister."

"Only she could be that evil."

"Yes. Because she adheres to dark practices."

"What do they want with Aly?"

"We'll talk about that later."

Jace is startled as Luther touches Hanna's shoulder and he closes the book; Luther turns to the crowd holding an athame, both hands above his head.

"Brothers and sisters," he begins, and onlookers of hundreds turn in the crowd like a domino effect. Suddenly a portly man with red hair bursts forth yielding a microphone, "I'm Chris," he says happily, "I'm a reporter for the *Pagan Tribune.* I'm here to cover the festival," he explains, yielding the microphone to his lips.

"Thank you," Luther says, "dear brothers and sisters," he continues, "we are no longer in hiding – we are gathered here together as Wiccan and Pagans, Witches and Warlocks, or as my dear cousin used to say – Folklore – because magic cannot be real."

And they all revel in laughter.

Luther smiles slightly.

"Who is your High Priestess?" One of them says.

"My beautiful departed cousin, Sterling Silver," he gasps, "she was killed in the company of the Priestess of Darkness. Who may call herself a Goddess."

"A Priestess?" She says, "for what Coven?"

"They have no name."

"That's unfortunate."

"Most sad news," another woman says, "how may we be of service to you?"

"A child has been stolen." Hanna sobs.

"The child bares the mark of protection," Luther says. "There is no secret here," he explains, squeezing her shoulder tight, "we ask for a following … to get her back."

"But who are we up against?"

"Her own twin sister."

The crowd gasps in unison.

"How is that so?" The first woman says.

"She is the Priestess of the Dark, possibly the dark lord – together they form a trinity of Lord, Priestess and Guardian."

"What is it that they want?"

"Followers. And power."

"But what with the child?" The second woman says.

"We only know what is written in the Prophecy … the blood of the Goddess of War and the Prince of Peace who inhabit the mortal body. Shed over the highest summit – the unison of the unholy wish to exterminate the holy trinity of Goddess, Prince and Child."

"Is the child holy?"

"The child bares the mark of unity."

"Then the child is a holy vessel."

"Yes."

"She is my daughter." Hanna exhales.

"You are too young to be a Priestess."

"I am her mother."

"Hanna is a Pagan," Lucius says and she turns in his direction.

Lucius, age nineteen, and the son of Luther, nods.

"That she is," Luther says, "a student of my dear cousin."

Hanna smiles faintly and takes the *Book of Prophecy* in her hands, "I need this," she says, "to be better prepared."

"I can help you," Lucius says.

"She doesn't need your help," Jace spats.

"Easy young bloke," Luther says.

"She does and will need help," Lucius says.

He begins to radiate light and Hanna is attracted to the energy.

"You're Lucius?" She says.

"Yes," he says, "you remember my name?"

"Well," she grins, "I can't remember all twenty names."

He grins, "I can help you with that as well."

"Then you're the upmost appreciated," Jace sniggers.

"We ask for a following to the North, to the highest summit at Mount Katahdin where the Goddess of Storms may be waiting."

"How long do we have?" The first woman says.

"Winter Samhain – the Winter Solstice – when the full cycle reaches one year."

"Then what?" Hanna says.

"They'll never get that far," Lucius says.

"How far?" She asks.

"To spill blood. To make him eternal."

"That monster? My daughter?"

"Yes. I'm so sorry."

"Promise me."

"I promise," He says, taking her hand, placing it to his chest, "we have all sworn to you."

"And I to you," she says, "tell me what is next?"

"We keep going. We build an army. And we beat them."

"Where? How?"

"We move on further North," Luther explains, "by foot, we walk, and we talk with those who care to listen."

"We hear you," the onlooker says, "tell us where. When."

"Look for the Raven…"

"No," Hanna says, "the Ravens are a dark army, but one."

"Look for the dark cat," Vienna pipes in.

"What cat?" Luther says.

"The Sister's Coven," Vienna says, "the emerald amulet …."

"My dog has one of those," Jace says, stepping to the side, to reveal Thor behind his legs.

"The Sisters were protecting him," Hanna says.

"So he wouldn't be confiscated," Vienna explains.

"They tried to help my daughter."

"Then you can follow the guidance of both," Elusha says.

"They are of service to the light," Gladys says.

"Then we shall alarm you with the call of…"

"Rajah and Thor," Hanna says.

The onlookers bow their heads and give their voices to the power of consecration to protect them; they offer their possessions they anointed, blessed and enchanted.

For Hanna an onlooker offers her locket that bares a single crystal she says can be used to call for her service. The name Reese she will not forget, and the festival brought on two hundred followers who set up camp in a clearing in Massachusetts.

Six

Lucius parks his tent next to Hanna and digs for his parka from within the duffle bag. He retrieves a canteen from inside his small hut of a tent and begins making hot chocolate over the fire; the circumference of the entire field is aligned with burning flames and a large fire at the center burns a pile of brush and debris. Hanna thinks about Sterling, but decides to be social.

"Are you nomadic?" She asks, huddling by the burning pit Lucius had made.

"We have a different lifestyle," he begins, "we Wiccans…"

"Where do you live? Or where are you from?"

"I'm from the land down under, but my mum brought me to the US when I was just five. She had a job here. In sales. But I don't remember much."

"Did something happen to her?"

"She died. A car accident. Been raised here by my father ever since. I was eight."

"Luther is your father?"

"That's right," he says, bringing her a hot cup of chocolate cocoa.

"Thank you."

"You might want to let it cool down. Might be a tad hot." He smiles.

"You practice Witchcraft with your father?"

"I was brought up by a group of men, the Warlocks mostly. Didn't know about practicing magic until I was twenty."

"What can you do?"

"I can make fire," he laughs, "as you see here."

Jace spats a cud to the earth and enters his tent.

"Doesn't take much to light a fire," Hanna says.

"Does it not? I mean I just whittle two twigs together, old Indian way, and make it burn with my hands."

"But I mean what can you do with Witchcraft?"

"Well of course you do. You have to excuse me – I'm into fires – it's quite cool out tonight."

"Rather bitter if you ask me."

Thor pants by the fire and lets out a sigh as he stretches his thick furry body. Jace kicks up a nearby bucket and spats again.

"Don't mind him," Hanna says patiently.

"Who is he to you? If you don't mind me asking."

"He's my daughter's father."

"The infant girl who was stolen…"

"A newborn really."

"I'm sorry. Are you two…?"

"No, we are not. He just promised to help me find her."

"Does he practice magic?"

"No, he does not."

"Have you?"

"I've only just begun."

"Well, I can help you learn."

"Thank you. Sterling said I was very intuitive. That I could see in the minds of others."

"Then I can help you fine tune your craft," he says, poking the fire.

"How?"

"You know, Sterling is my father's cousin; my father was, or is, her mother's brother."

"Unfortunately we didn't get to know one another for long," she says, rubbing her hands over the fire, sipping from the cup of cocoa, "I can't help but feel so guilty."

"Nonsense. I think she knew but couldn't conceive of it."

"She said she wasn't certain what a monster her twin sister had become."

"And now family must fight family. It's why my father is connected but he's involved to save the light."

"How can he, or we, do that?"

"The light took on a mortal body. That means the darkness is getting stronger."

"But now they have stolen her…"

"But it's not that easy. There are laws, plus the right time and place."

"The Fall Equinox?"

"No. The Winter Solstice."

"My daughter's birthday…"

"The Solstice?"

"Yes."

"Then the light is most strong with her."

Lucius motions with his hands for her to sit down beside the fire, away from the stream of smoke, to get warmer. Together they roast meats over the fire to keep their bodies strong. He removes an athame from his pocket and the light reflects from its steel blade. "Sometimes," he says, "you can see the future reflected from this blade."

Hanna takes the carving knife he uses to whittle the wood and peers at the shining reflective metal. Lucius begins to chant the dissonant sound *Om* and the Hawk and the Raven soar overhead.

Her eyelids become heavy and they drop slightly under the humming of the sacred mantra.

"I only see the sky," she says, "filled with bats."

"What are they doing?"

"Swarming. Like the Ravens had, the night Sterling…" And her voice trails off and she becomes more lucid, "I saw a witch," she says, "an old woman, predicting the future with Runes… she has my baby."

"It's possible Goldie doesn't excel in psychic ability and is using her to guide her."

"She uses telekinesis…"

"That's likely how…"

"She stole my baby."

"And bi-location."

"Yes. I suppose. So she is powerful?"

"She's a sneak. An evil one."

"Then we must…"

"Be vigilant. Here," he says, "take my athame; it's rarely used for cutting but it can help you to see…"

"The future?"

"Maybe only what is happening in the precise moment."

At that moment the four sisters appear huddling around the fire.

"Hello, Lucius," Amber says.

"Hanna." Sydney says.

"Hi," Lucius says curiously.

"Your mind is marvelous," Sydney says, pulling off the hood to her large fur coat.

"Whatever do you mean?" He snickers.

"Sydney can read minds," Hanna explains.

"Come off it." He says.

"Yes." Sydney smiles.

"We are three covens deep," Priscilla says.

"And a couple hundred followers," Paisley adds.

"We must have a strong army," Lucius says.

"Strength in numbers," Amber says.

Hanna conceals the athame in her cargo pocket and heads into her tent for a night of sleep – if she can stop thinking.

With the rising sun they all begin to travel the distance on a hundred mile stretch into the mountain peaks of the White Mountains. In the remote space of the mountains lives a tribe of Druids and Sister Covens whose men are skilled in the arts of battle; having learned their trade in military strategy they took to the mountains where they practice daily knowing the battle of darkness lies in the sacred text; the alpine jungle yields coverage for their covens.

There are thru hikers along the trail; some stop to ask where such a large army of men and women are deploying but, Luther merely mentions taking a hike into Maine to enjoy the scenic route and the ice caps of the White Mountains that only winter can bring.

Many of the hikers show interest in joining and one of them, Bernard Alexander, recognizes the totem birds atop the trees. He points at his own guide, a three-legged cat purring beneath his large overcoat; he stands like a giant, or some wilderness beast, with great white hair and an unkempt beard past his chin. He and Luther make great friends and he confides in the stranger that they follow the ancient text.

"The pending war," Bernard says, nodding, as he takes strides with Luther who introduces him to Lucius and Hanna.
Bernard explains how he was a cadet in the Army and had led men through war in Vietnam. He also speaks of the secret Army of the mountains, inquiring if they are to go there.

"Yes," Luther says, as they shake hands – Luther knowing that this beast of a man can lead him to the Army of the United Covens.
The Army Staff Sergeant, Bernard Alexander, speaks of the hidden Army and vows to defeat any dark presence that seeks power over the light of the Gods.

They stop at a small tavern to each take their turn at filling their canteen or flask as they choose. Hanna huddles by the indoor fire to defeat frostbite and changes her socks. Sage pecks at the window from outside and the Raven caws in the distance.

Lucius accompanies Hanna by the fire with a goblet of wine in each hand.

"Just what I needed," Hanna says with a tear in her eye and Jace storms off.

"I never got the name of Sterling's Raven," she sobs, as Lucius wipes a tear with his forefinger.

"Why the tear?" He asks, "Are you going to be okay, darling?"

"I need my daughter." She exhales.

"Clover." He says.

"I'm sorry?"

"Her Raven is named Clover. Like a lucky four leaf clover."

"Now that is folklore," she forces a smile.

He taps his goblet to hers, "The Warlock's Coven vows to defeat them and get her back."

"I need to hold her again."

"I want to help you do that."

"How?"

"We must train."

"Tell me more," she says, taking a seat as the couple hundred joiners file into the tavern as they flock to the open basement that houses a bar and dining space; the Witches and the Warlocks dine with ale or cider, red wine and bread with cheese. For a moment some of them can forget about the war but not Hanna, who sobs lightly so she goes unnoticed by the joiners and the Covens.

The leaders Luther and Bernard can be seen seated at the bar, likely discussing strategy and technique in holy wars – how best to use magic before a blade can cause ruin to a coven or how to know when to use brute strength in place of magic.

Hanna appears in deep thought when Lucius takes her hand into his, "I'd give anything to just end this war now and have her back in your arms."

Jace glares from the window, spatting at the ground where he stands and takes leave with Thor trailing behind.

"I wish like anything that you could do that right now."

"Does her father feel the same?"

"He's never met his daughter."

"That says a lot. And nothing at the same time."

"He swore he would help me get her back."

For this night the Covens and Pagans are warm from the cold as they set up camp surrounding the tavern where fires burn illuminating their faces when Hanna sees the face of Sterling in the candlelight.

"I may not be here in body but I am here in the soul," she begins as her image reflects from the wall in the light of an anointed candle.

"Sterling," Hanna says from the corner of the tavern as Lucius searches the flame for a face.

"Where?" He asks.

"Her astral body, illuminated from the wall, can you see her face?"

"I'm looking but I can't see anything."

"I can speak with you in séance too but for now just keep Clover with you and Sage too. Be sure not to alienate Jace. You need all the help you can get now," she says, as the front door opens, allowing the cold winter breeze to flood the room with Thor at his side and Lucius takes leave with a nod allowing them to talk over the fire.

Seven

In the twilight hours, Lucius wakes Hanna from her small two man tent.

"I couldn't help but overhear your conversation last night." He whispers.

Only the night guards are awake as Richard, Matthew, Bill and Ned have third duty to tend the fires and secure the perimeters.

"So he now wants what he had but can no longer have?"

"That's the gist of our conversation," she says, groggily, yawning.

"I couldn't sleep. I thought all night about you."

"But you need your sleep for the hike."

"Sorry, I just had to ask…"

"I know." She says, grabbing her clothes from the pile.

They spend the morning hours packing their camp style gear and drinking hot cider. During the hike along the thousands-mile trail, Lucius keeps pace aside Hanna while Jace and Thor flank their sides.

Luther and Bernard lead the pack; Bernard's cat is packed warmly in a duffle bag. They head for a clearing in the White Mountains that is surrounded by alpine in a depression complete with a lake; the Druids live there among their families where they build their own cabins and are said to train daily for the coming of a war as described in the *Book of Prophecy,* written by early prophetic witches but by whom, the dark or the light, is not clearly known.

Jace bunks by a fallen tree and opens the book to study its contents; within the pages it reads that the coming of the war begins with great winds and he thinks about Hanna's talk of Leisha, the Guardian of the North, where the Prophecy claims the war will take place. He thinks of Goldie and the Prophecy and the Goddess of Storms; together Goldie and Leisha nurture the prophetic war as accomplices of evil. He then reads on about the rulers of the outer worlds – the Goddess of Celestial Light, the Prince of Peace and the dark ruler who Hanna describes as a beast. Its contents are otherwise vague and the omitted details makes him uneasy.

"How can magic protect you?" He eyes Lucius.

"People all around us here are adept in magic also known as magical surrealism... some are born with innate instincts and abilities, many of those abilities are termed ESP, or that of extra senses past the primary senses; others are even more adept and can shape shift, levitate or become a light body and travel the cosmos. The amount of protection one witch has against another depends on their intention and level of skill … just like sparring in the martial arts."

"And that's where we are heading?"

"Yes, to the hidden army whose skills will aid us in the battle against the dark rulers."

"So you're wizards? They'll teach us to wave wands?"

"If magic came from sticks we would all be adept witches, but it's not that easy. The power comes from within – like accessing or using parts of the brain that are not typically used in basic consciousness. You will learn how to access those areas of the brain that can make you skilled in the esoteric arts. Something like witchcraft."

"And how will witchcraft stop a blade or a bullet?"

"Imagine your body becoming an astral body, levitating, using telekinesis to divert a bullet – it's all the reason for training.

"Then we become brothers."

"Then we become brothers." He nods.

"That witch has our daughter," Jace says.

"And I will help you get her back."

Jace forces a smile.

After twenty minutes to break from the hike they set out again by foot toward the Druids

Army where they hope to find elusive Pagans and Wiccans.

Vienna, Gladys and Elusha flank the trail with The Warlock's Coven at their side; twenty grown men, some young and some old, keep stride with their animal guides. Jade stays protected within the emerald lockets. Sage and Clover remain strong leading at the front of the couple hundred followers and practitioners who file in lines like a military brigade.

The few hundred will become thousands as they locate the many covens that believe in and practice the art of divination. They enter a clearing that is surrounded by a lush canopy of pine; cabins are abundant like an outdoor oasis. The views are of the peaks of the White Mountains of New Hampshire.

In that moment, the practitioners are in awe. Bernard knocks on the door of the home with a red tin roof and a wraparound porch, but no one answers. He makes his way to the back of the house when a loud sound like thunder can be heard in the distance, Bernard bellows a loud yell and Luther, along with four of the coven, make for the mountains. From the clearing all looks picturesque but among the tree line there are men hidden among the brush when they attack from all sides baring great staffs with a knob at the end like a balled-up fist. The Druids' Army is in full attack, cornering the sisters, upholding Lucius, pressing bodies into the earth onto their stomachs. Another bang like thunder sounds from the distance when Bernard shows in the clearing, waving his arms, "Hold it right there!" He hollers over the commotion of hundreds of men detaining their followers. "We are here in peace!"

The army flanks the clearing on both sides of the frozen lake when there's another bang but much closer this time; a robust, stout man, yielding a musket enters the clearing and Bernard whistles when Thor and Sage circle their humans who are laid out on the cold earth by the Druids' Army.

"Bernard?" The stout man with the dark hair hollers as he waves the musket overhead, "Let them go," he says, "damn lucky I recognized ya!" He says, "My army was forewarned of an oncoming attack."

"Forewarned by who?" Bernard asks.

"By two women. Says they have a witch, an ancient in the arts, who saw my army attacked on our own land."

The Pagans stand to their feet and dust the snow off their beards. Jace nudges Thor by the collar; the emerald stone shines in a glittery color of jade, like the eyes of the cat.

"Warned you like she warned me," Jace says. "They assured the army that the following was only interested in taking possessions – leaving nothin' and no one untouched."

"Have you heard of the prophecy?"Jace says, removing the book from his knapsack and Hanna steps forward.

"They are the ones who have stolen a child!" She exhales.

"The prophecy is why you are here?" One yells from the distance.

"To gather an army, a following," Luther steps forward, "to defeat the darkness."

"Those women have stolen my daughter."

"Stolen?" The stout man says.

"Protected by the witch they claimed was to warn you."

"You are all lucky to be alive," he says, "had you not found Bernard we were to defeat the coming of the most powerful evil…"

"They deceived you. All of you." Bernard says.

Lucius takes Hanna by the hand and pulls her onto the clearing, "This is the child's mother," he says, "the same woman who stole her also murdered my father's cousin."

"Our sister coven," Luther says.

"By what name?"

"And who are you accompanied with here?"

"We are The Warlock's Coven – a lot of twenty, and there are The Sister's Coven, the

Guardians, and a couple hundred practitioners in the art of Witchcraft."

"For what purpose?"

"First, can I get a name?" Luther asks.

"This is Archibald," Bernard says, "and this is Luther," he continues, "please, both of you, do shake hands. We are all friends here."

The men exchange a friendly greeting, before asking, "How may we be of any help?"

Archibald scans the bodies before him, seeing no weapons and places the musket over his shoulder.

Jace hands the Prophecy to Hanna and she reads from its pages: the coming of the dark lord is disguised in lies and deceit. Do not be fooled by double standards. The enemy stays near and only refrains from harm until the time he seeks power.

"There appears to be no evil here," Archibald says, and he waves as his army advances without arms.

"Evil is with those women and the beast they protect," Luther says.

"What is this beast?"

"Something with pointed teeth, long fingers and toes like talons and wings of leather like a bat," Hanna says, closing the book's pages.

"The prophecy speaks of an impending war," Jace says, as Lucius slits his eyes toward his father.

"The war is among two opposing forces in nature. Held before the Goddess of Celestial Light and the Goddess of Storms," Luther says.

"In the North," Hanna says.

"At the highest summit," Lucius adds.

"That's the summit of Mount Katahdin," Hanna continues.

"Where is this?" Archibald inquires.

"The highest point North. In Maine," Luther explains.

"Where the Goddess of Storms resides with the Guardian of the North," Hanna explains.

"She's no Goddess," Jace spats.

"The point of most power," Luther says.

"Then shouldn't we make this less easy on them?" Archibald says.

"We?" Luther says.

The Druids' Army laughs, their women come onto the porches from their houses.

"We are familiar with the prophecy. We know this is a serious matter for an army."

"Not just any army," Bernard says.

"That's correct. An army of Warlocks who have knowledge…"

"Who are adept in witchcraft," Archibald finishes. "All is well ladies," he hollers.

"Then would anyone like some ale? Hot cider?" His wife hollers back. Her face shows age but her body is lean and strong. She wears a shawl made of wool. Past the clearing there is a farm nestled among the mountains.

"I'm sure we all could use a hot meal," he hollers back.

"The whole lot?"

"Each family can house our guests. We have over two hundred houses," he says.

And she scans the clearing seeing the men and women who have come there – some are bleeding.

"Certainly dear," she says.

And the night brings ale, wine, meat and breads with cheese.

They feast.

Eight

The Sister's Coven, Hanna and Jace, Luther and his son Lucius, Richard, Matthew, Bill and Ned of the Warlock's Coven, and Bernard, along with the three Guardians, bunk at the home of Archibald and Diana Wilt in a spacious six thousand square foot home in the Druids' Town.

The following morning is productive. They file in uniform rows to begin what will be a daily routine of learning fine motor skills through the art of Thai Chi. When they move on to weaponry, Hanna removes her athame and holds it in front of her when Lucius motions with a single finger on the blade.

"The athame isn't for cutting, only for divination," he explains, "wait to see what they have to give you." He winks, and she places the athame in its holster and into her cargo pocket.

The women of the Druids' Army file out of their two hundred homes that surround the clearing; they fall into place onto the battle field as the men open a great storage container that houses muskets, bayonets, wooden staffs with mullets on the tips and swords of shining reflective metal. It's not just the men who bring out the heavy artillery; the women remove a mace from beneath their skirts and then the mock battle begins.

"Lines on the left," Archibald yells, "defend yourselves," and they raise an arm for the block as the first weapon they use is the mace with the women in offense. Diana is lean and strong as she shows great stamina bringing the mace toward Lucius; he ducks, weaves, bends, and in the end, levitates.

"Well done," Diana says, and Lucius looks at Hanna who stands bleeding from the nose and mouth; a large whistle sounds and the following of practitioners stand in defeat; some with broken limbs and others limping with pain.

"And that," Archibald exhales, "is how to lose a war." He grins.

The participants shake hands to extend their respect.

"But tomorrow, we practice." He says.

Jace is the first to stammer from the line as he hangs his head, holding his nose, and Thor leaps at his side.

"What the hell was that?" Jace grimaces.

"How to lose a war," Hanna repeats.

The Guardians and the Sisters walk away unscathed.

In the evening the sun lowers over the western mountain as Lucius closes the door to the red-tin-roof log cabin with the cedar siding illuminated by hues of pink and purple over the horizon.

Vienna wrings a hot rag over the faucet and places it to Jace's left eye. "Thanks," he manages to say with a lopsided grin.

"She got you pretty good," Gladys says, placing bandages to his knuckles.

"I'm fine, really," he says, cringing.

"This may not be a war for non-practitioners," Lucius huffs.

"Precisely why we practice," Diana says, entering the kitchen with a platter full of vegetables in tow, "All of us," she says.

"How can three hundred people learn magic overnight?" Jace spats.

"I was under the impression that only a few haven't learned the Craft," she smiles.

"Certainly worth a try, is it not?" Lucius says.

"It sure is," Luther says, taking a seat at the dinner table.

"More than worth it," Archibald says, "to my understanding," he begins…

"Archibald Richard," Diana threatens, with a raised brow.

"It's just my understanding you've lost a child."

"Yeah," Jace says.

"He's never met her," Amber says, entering into the kitchen, sneering.

"He's making amends," Sydney says, with one arm to her shoulder.

"She's in the possession of that hag," Jace spats. When the day washes to night and the morning is rigorous; sparring between Jace and Lucius never looked so grim.

With Lucius commanding a front kick, Jace is to levitate without stumbling.

"You have to see it," Lucius yells.

"Feel it," Amber yells.

"Mind focus. Body focus." Luther adds.

Jace takes the defensive position with both fists in the ready, and defends a roundhouse kick with a double arm block.

"Now, feel it more," Archibald says, as the circle of Pagans close in and follow Lucius' lead, "you have to feel the weight of your body become suspended in air," Lucius says as the two hundred practitioners of witchcraft follow suit.

"Breathe deep, and exhale a slow breath, become buoyant – feel the ground beneath your feet."

Lucius moves with a jumping kick to Jace's right side as he moves swiftly like a cat – he breathes rhythmically and jumps, hollering as another roundhouse kick pierces his side, as Lucius spars with great fists and Jace does a forward roll and launches to his feet.

"Nice move," Lucius says, "but let me see you catch some air."

"Ride it like the wind," Vienna hollers from outside the circle.

Jace does a back flip as he learned in gymnastics training.

"That's the way of the warrior," Luther guffaws.

"Don't let me stop you," Lucius says with a front kick and a left sided fist – Jace jumps, taking the path of least resistance, soaring through the air, in a front flip with both knees braced at his chest, he hovers for a solid moment, over his opponent, and lands behind his back.

"You have coveted the way of the warrior," Luther grins.

Lucius gives him a slap on the back.

"Next is dodging a bullet," Lucius smiles.

The Pagans clap and whistle with enthusiasm.

"The way of the Pagans is to feel the way, with all of your senses through mind, through attention, through focus and coordination – and never undermine the passion," Luther says.

"With the passion for the art," Archibald agrees, and Bernard nods in recognition.

From the tree line the landscape turns to dark as the clouds cover the sun – overhead the sky becomes engulfed with bats as the Pagans stop their sparring and a haggard cackle is heard like a strong wind.

"You cannot win a war with the likes of you," she haggles them as the bats flutter their papery wings; the women use the mace to shield their faces from razor sharp teeth.

"You give her back you hag!" Jace screams, removing a blade from its sheath, when he's toppled by Lucius who forces him to the ground.

"Not here. Not now," Lucius exclaims with force.

And the laughter of a dark voice – the Guardians' personal witch – can be heard like a concert speaker.

"You will never defeat the dark," her voice cackles again as she taunts them, in a hollow laugh; with the sun seeping through the dark the bats enter a great black hole like a vortex of immense circular motion and vanish entirely. And all becomes quiet again.

"That old hag is toying with us!" Jace screams.

"She's an evil hell," Marcus says.

"Like a devil," Archibald says.

"If witches believed such things," Lucius says.

"What do witches believe?" Luther asks.

"There's no evil, just the forces of nature," Lucius says.

"Controlled by a witch," Jace spats.

"But not by the right kind," Marcus says.

"She has no good intentions. We all know," Bernard says, "not all witches follow celestial magic."

"No witch should control the forces of nature to seek power and control," Luther says.

"Then tell her that," Jace glowers.

Hanna reaches for his arm but he pulls away. "I can't process this shit right now," He screams.

With the beginning of the rain he notices a rainbow beyond the horizon.

"Rain in February," Luther says.

"Just to add to the ice," Archibald shakes his head.

"Then we use it to our advantage," Lucius says.

"Training continues tomorrow," Luther says. They take leave to the cabins while feeling the pains of winter in their bones.

In the evening that ensues, Jace hears a knock on his bedroom door in the one of many rooms the expansive home provides; the home reminds him of a convent but made of cedar as he glares at the window looking below at the Raven tapping below on the window sill and in the deep forest, he feels and senses eyes, gleaming.

He answers the door to find Elusha dressed in a sleek evening gown.

"Hello," she says, with a wide smile before she barges into the room, drawing the curtain closed. She turns subtly about the room, peering with wide eyes, "You have a sound mind," she says, and takes a seat at the corner bunk.

"I'm sorry?" He says, "I don't follow you."

"You were able to defend yourself against a fellow witch," she smiles a wide, toothy grin.

"Right. But I'm not really a witch."

"No?" She says, "But you do so well," she muffles, peering serenely into his eyes.

"I guess. But it's just because I was a gymnast," he says, awkwardly.

"A witch could certainly use those skills as you have."

"The movements were useful I guess," he says, frankly.

"Tell me," she says, crossing one leg over the other, "how do you feel about, you know, your girlfriend?"

"My girlfriend?" He sniggers, "you mean Hanna?"

"That's right," she says, and the Raven can be heard cawing.

"What's up with Clover?" He chides.

"Never mind that," she squirms.

"Stupid bird." He says, with a slanted grin.

"Tell me," she continues, "are you two in love?"

"That's a loaded question," he sniggers, with the shrug of his shoulders, "but no. I definitely don't think so."

"Oh, no?" She says, "Pity."

"Why do you care?" He sneers.

"I'm a stickler for young love, and you know, all things beautiful."

"Then I'd say ask Lucius," he says, taking a step back.

"Lucius?" She exhales, "but are you certain?" She says, leaning forward, her breath onto his cheek.

Jace slits his eyes at the *Book of Prophecy* that peaks from the other corner of the bed, at the page he had just torn.

"I answered your question. So now maybe you can answer mine."

"Go on."

"What's love have to do with the book of prophecy?"

"Why do you ask?" She says, standing.

"It's the reason we are all here," he explains, "the book says that love can be salvation or else... but then the page is torn ... so I wondered if you could tell me more."

"Oh, not at all," she says, pulling the curtain open to find the eye of the Hawk peering from the forest, and there's a knock on the door. "Now who is it?" He says, as Elusha vanishes from where she stands – as does the Raven from the window sill.

Hanna knocks on the door again, this time more forcefully, and she opens the door, grabs him by the arm, "Come quickly," she says, Luther has something to say to us.

Outside, the Covens, Guardians and the followers are assembled.

"Something has happened," Luther says, loudly as Lucius takes Hanna's side, "half the followers have disappeared from the area," he whispers.

"So has Clover," Hanna says.

"Our following has diminished," Luther says, "if any of you have an idea of where and how..."

He is interrupted by a woman from the crowd, "They have fallen to darkness," she clamors.

"How do you know this?" Says Luther.

"There was a woman who possessed them..." she continues, "a Guardian!"

"Elusha is missing," Vienna screams.

"It cannot be so!" Gladys cries.

"We have only two Guardians," Luther says.

"And now only a hundred at the most in the following," Archibald says.

"But the Druids' Army, your army, is hundreds strong," Bernard says.

"But where are the rest?" Luther says, "We have merely half of the lot here."

"Vermont," Archibald responds.

"Then we continue on," Luther says.

"When it is time," Archibald says. Jace throws remnants of paper into the fire, "So what if she's on Goldie's side," he says, brushing his fingers through his hair, "So what if she… if she seduced them!"

"What is this?" Luther says.

"How do you know of this?" Lucius says.

"I don't," Jace says, turning toward the night.

Nine

During the month of March a blizzard has them bound to the White Mountains of New Hampshire. From the clearing, Hanna enters the forest where she finds pine branches littered with snow. She removes the athame from her pocket and drives it into a fallen limb. With one hand to its blade and the other extended toward the darkened sky she bellows – "Guardian hear me!" As the thick clouds shroud the sky a single lightning bolt emerges from the blade and strikes the evening sky. The jolt of electricity forces Hanna against a sturdy tree and from the blade she sees Goldie's face pierce through the reflective metal, "I have already one," she hisses and the view of Jace settling by the fire morphs into view as Sydney climbs through a vortex parting the image into two.

"He's hiding something," Sydney exhales as she grabs at the blade with another surge of lightning piercing the ever-darkening sky and Goldie sounds again, "Come to me foolish one," she glowers as the sky parts; her face emerges from the black, billowing clouds and she smiles a wry grin.

"Never evoke a Guardian or Spirit alone," Sydney says.

"She's none of those things," Hanna says, forcing herself upon the blade, "she's just an evil witch," she screams into the omnipresent sky.

"Hanna!" Sydney says, as Vienna and Gladys emerge from the snowy banks.

"Never evoke them!" Gladys says.

"I wanted to see my daughter!" Hanna screams.

"But you are too bold, dear," Gladys holds her.

"You have no need to do this alone," Vienna says.

"Well here you all are," Hanna says, "I'm never alone," she whispers.

"As you shouldn't be," Gladys says.

She peers at the face of Goldie among the clouds as they all grab for the blade in unison and extract it from the cold earth leaving Goldie to disappear – her wry face fading, still laughing. All that remains is an image of Jace beside the fire and from the light upon the wall Sterling's face comes into view, "None of you can go out alone," she says, as Hanna, the Guardians and Sydney step toward her image in their view, "We do not know what my sister seeks," she says, extending a hand to Hanna who reaches for her, "Goldie may only be beaten by the numbers as she has a great following," she whispers as the flames dance from the chimney and the image begins to die.

"Is she the Goddess of Storms?" Hanna says.

"She follows all that is dark," Sterling says, "together with the Guardian of Earth and Fire she has great power. She seeks to be High Priestess and perhaps too the Goddess of darkness."

"She exhibits control over the elements," Gladys says.

"But sister," Vienna says, "we are the Guardians over the East and the West and the elements of Air and Water."

"They have control of Earth and Fire," Gladys says.

"You can control the elements?" Hanna quivers.

"That's what Guardians do, dear," Gladys explains, "Leisha is the ruler of the North and Guardian of Earth."

"And Elusha is Guardian of the South," Vienna explains, "and ruler of the element Fire."

"As Guardians you do control the elements."

"Yes," Gladys says.

"I can control water at my will," Vienna says.

"And I control the winds, or air," Gladys explains."

"It makes us a strong pair, but rulers of the Earth and Fire are also companion forces," Vienna says.

"Water puts out fire," Hanna says.

"In the literal," Vienna explains, "but not being on the same end of the spectrum we may cancel one another out."

"Why have the Guardians of Earth and Fire sided with Goldie? With the dark?"

"We do not know," Gladys says, disappointed.

As the women encircle one another, the remaining three of the Sister's Coven enter through the vortex.

"Are we in séance?" Amber says.

"No sisters," Sydney says, "we have come to Hanna in a time of need."

"What's happening?" Asks Priscilla.

"I summonsed the Guardians," Hanna says.

"That's evocation of horrible evil," Paisley says.

"I know," Hanna admits, placing the athame into her pocket.

"It will be best to séance in the company of adept witches from now on," Vienna says, and they all agree.

"It's my daughter the witch has taken," Hanna interjects, "and has left her in the care of another haggard old witch."

"She's no witch," Gladys says.

"We understand," Vienna says soothingly, "that's why we are here to help you."

Hanna simply nods and inhales a deep breath – trying to be calm and strong – for no other reason than her baby, as the view of firelight and Jace fades leaving Hanna to wonder.

Hanna knocks on the door to the men's guest house and finds Lucius dressed for the evening.

"I summonsed that bitch," she says, peering through the crack in the door; seeing no one else she barges inside.

"They say Jace may be keeping secrets," she says, taking a seat within the room.

"Elusha paid him a visit before she vanished with half the Army. He says she seduced them…"

"Maybe she hexed their drinking water," he smirks.

"I understand apprehension but she did appear to be too sultry. A seductress, like the deck of Major Arcana." He agrees, "Yes I know," he says, "she showed up here before she went missing too."

"What happened?"

"She wanted to know more about you and Jace. If you're intimately in love."

"Why would she care?"

"I don't know. But she tried peering into my eyes, like a vixen, with some kind of interest in my soul. I could feel her, intimately, like she was trying to suck the life out of me."

"Oh my, God."

"Yeah. It was intense."

"How did you escape her?"

"Jace. He came to my room… he just barged in… I think he thought …"

"That you may be betraying me?"

"I don't know for sure, but maybe. It did seem that way …. But he just barged in. Then he left, and that may be when she went to his room."

"She seduces men. To get answers."

"And to take their soul," Lucius agrees.

"Well, but what happens to…"

"Their body? It's as if they must evaporate. Leaving only a mere shadow of the man he used to be."

"Oh," she exhales, "in Aly's room – there had been a dark shadow, of a man."

"A discarnate."

"But what would he have been doing there? And who was he?"

"The dark must have been interested in her since before her birth… possibly the mark of protection was their interest."

"But it's just a symbol. Of the balance between light and dark."

"The dark has no interest in being equal with the light."

"So they stole her."

"Yes. And we think Goldie herself has done this."

"But does she not have a dark master? A ruler?"

"I don't know. Most we know is from the Book of Prophecy."

"Jace keeps that book. It was sent to us by Sterling."

"Most witches already know the prophecy, and don't need the book, but you and Jace are…"

"The newest in the Craft."

"That's right."

"Then what is your father planning to do?"

"All we know already – to build an Army and to try to defeat the dark Army."

"On the summit of Mount Katahdin…"

"And the ancient legend says that…"

"The Goddess of Storms…"

"Will reign over the mountain."

"Is that Goldie then?"

"Goldie might claim to be the High Priestess of Darkness but the Goddess of Storms reigns over the highest summit."

"Tell me," she says, taking his hand into hers, "about the Prince of Peace."

"The Prince of Peace," he stutters, "have you seen him?"

"Yes. With the Goddess of Celestial Light."

"In the same body?"

"Emanating from my daughter."

"Then she is in the possession of …"

"Yes," Hanna interjects, "both the Goddess of Light and the Prince of Peace…" She says, with a tear in her eye, "and there was one more…"

"Who? Or what?"

"The face of evil. A man. A dark man. With a gaunt face."

"I'm not sure I buy it," he says, pacing.

"You don't believe me?"

"I don't believe her."

"Who then?"

"Goldie. She appears to be acting solely on her own."

"Could he have been she?"

"Yes! As a body double. Shape shifting." He explains, "Did he speak?"

"Yes. And he appears in my dreams."

"But she's still a sneak. A liar," he bellows.

"Then she knew all along…"

"The dark shadow…"

"Then she did know…"

"Must have been one of her followers who found you."

"It's starting to make sense."

"Goldie was hiding her true identity from you."

"Then what is the monster that killed Sterling?"

"A Gargoyle. A pet."

"Gargoyle?"

"Only in ancient lore. But it's a beast of the dark forces."

"Then who do we…"

"Who do we kill?"

"Yes."

"My father may know. There's only so much that he has told me of the Prophecy."

"Can you think of anything else?"

"Yes. Yes I can."

"Tell me."

"Now that you have told me… now that I know more… that the Goddess and the Prince possess Aly…."

"Possess sounds like evil," she whispers.

"They inhabit her body. Like a spirit or a soul in the body of an incarnate."

"An incarnated child."

"Yes, but listen, we can split them … to save one of them… now."

"How do we do that?"

"There needs to be another body. Another birth."

"The prophecy… it says that if both forces of masculine and feminine inhabit only one body… they can split in two and inhabit another."

"How does this happen?"

"The unity of true love."

"True love?"

"The Celestial Light will shine in the body of the truest love."

"I see. But what about Aly?"

"Evil has not possessed her. We are lucky at the moment they care for her until they get what they want."

"What exactly do they want?"

"That's where the Prophecy is vague."

"So we know its power and war."

"Yes."

As the sun breaks over the mountain, Hanna wakes in Lucius' bed as the men file in after a day of hunting following last week's blizzard.

Hanna excuses herself from the room, wrapped in a white towel as the men smirk and nod.

"Enjoying some company, Lucius?" Luther says, placing a carving knife onto the table.

"Better question is – how did the hunting go?" He musters a smile.

"We have enough meat to last out this storm that's coming in," he says, and Lucius exits the room.

He enters the large entertaining area where the Druids' Army, the following, the Guardians, the four sisters and the Warlock's Coven convene over a hot meal. There is a large wrap-around porch that is enclosed and heated where guests have a panoramic view of the jutted White Mountains. Lucius grabs a plate of freshly stewed meat and a chilled glass of Pale Ale and heads to the seating area on the deck. He meets Hanna who is already dining there as she blushes slightly and he leans over to kiss atop her head. He knows that his father is planning to train more heavily once they leave for Vermont where they intend to find the second half of the Druids' Army who have also been training for the Holy War. The Druids speak of them as a brother Army who resides at the Mountain of Pico Peak at the Northern-most summit.

His father has told him of the trainings that occur there in the Green Mountains; Lucius suspects they will travel there through the summer when training won't have to withstand brutal weather. Lucius and Hanna exchange glances before he reaches for her neck, bringing her head to his shoulder.

"It's just a matter of time," he says.
"I pray this works," she says.
"We pray. But we also prepare." He whispers as they watch the crowd before them who talk over the fire, who mingle and who share in love and gratitude.
Jace approaches, nods to Lucius, who excuses himself to the far end of the room with Jace, where Hanna sees that he removes

the Prophecy, hands it to Lucius and walks away.

He returns to Hanna and hands her the book, "He wants you to have it," he says.

"Why couldn't he just bring the book to me himself?"

"It's a band of brothers pact," Lucius explains, "like a brother's code of conduct."

"Like a possession?"

"Like family."

"Oh."

"He knows it will never be between the two of you again."

"Nope. He lost me." She smiles.

"And I have found you," Lucius says.

"And now we find Aly," she says.

Ten

Hanna lies back in her bed with the side table light on; she reads through the *Book of Prophecy* scanning its pages for any hint as to how she can get her daughter back in her arms. She peers over the words: Dark Army, War, Cold Winds, Power, Raging Storms, The Battle of the Two Worlds, Evil Dominion – but nowhere in the text does she read about a baby, a kidnapping, or any hint at what they want with her baby. She reads the text from front to back, thumbing the edges of torn pages wondering what is written there; on the bottom crease of the last torn page is only one word: Love.

What does a war have to do with love? She wonders as she examines the text for any sign of answers when she touches the crystal upon her neck and she remembers Reese from the Pagan Pride Festival – thinking that perhaps she has the answers. She sits with crossed legs holding onto the stone and calls for her by name.

"Reese, Reese, Reese," she says, in a chanted monotone, "by the power of three come to me…"

With her eyes closed she first sees Reese in her mind's eye while keeping one hand on the locket a voice calls to her, "Open your eyes," she says and Reese appears in the flesh; the flesh is more refined unlike the blurred edges of the spirit. Hanna peers at her serene face that is round with brown hair to the chin that is tucked behind her ear.

"A body double?" Hanna says, uncertain.

"No." She says simply, "I teleport fairly easily. I was waiting for you to call on me."

"You were?"

"Yes. The reason I gave you the crystal."

"Do you know why I have called on you?"

"To know more of the Prophecy."

"There is something very particular I'm curious about."

"Love?" She says modestly.

"How do you know this? What do you know?"

"That she is incapable of feeling love. That she has blocked her soul from feeling the inception of love."

"What else?"

"She was incapable of loving her very own sister."

"Do you know Sterling?"

"Yes. I was a friend. A distant friend, but she knew we all could be found in Boston."

"Her creature…"

"Murdered Sterling. Yes. By Goldie's will alone. He is a dark creature that is a totem for only one ruler."

"How can she rule anything?"

"By being the Highest Priestess who likely follows a powerful demon, but one that she has created, who reigns over the darkness."

"Is that why she murdered her own sister?"

"Yes. She is bound to the dark by showing no love."

"But it also could be love that defeats her."

"My love?"

"Say no more. If she has your mind you don't want her to lead us on any diversions."

With that message her voice becomes dim, "I must go now," she says, "but I will be ahead of you in Vermont."

Her image becomes dim as a portal opens and she vanishes into the vortex that is shrouded with light. A few shards of white light energy sparkles about the room and Hanna extends her fingertips to catch them like snowflakes. And with the snap of fingers the lights go out. In the darkness her very own heavy breathing is all that can be heard followed by the crying of a baby. "Aly," Hanna screams, "Aly," she says, extending her arms in all directions when she hears the cackle of the Hag – "Come to me," the witch says.

"Give me my daughter," Hanna says, beginning to weep.

"Oh, poor, poor pitiful child," the Hag murmurs in the darkness when Hanna reaches the light switch, and Lucius, followed by Jace, bursts into the room.

"We could hear you screaming," Lucius says.

"What happened?" Jace says.

"The Hag. She was here. Her voice … I could hear Aly crying." She sobs.

"Okay," Lucius says, "stay calm, she's just using telepathy…"

"She turned off the lights."

"She's toying with you."

"What did the hag say?" Jace bellows.

"Come to me. I think."

"You think?"

"I know."

"She won't succeed over my dead body," Jace spats, appearing furious.

"There can't be death," Lucius says, "only victory over evil…"

"If that's in the prophecy," Hanna says.

"It's not," Jace yells.

"But the pages have been torn," Hanna murmurs.

"There's nothing useful in the damn book," Jace says forcefully, "forget the book." He says, slitting his eyes and leaving the room.

"What could it be?" Hanna asks.

"What," says Lucius.

"Sydney says he's hiding something."

"Only his own heart," Lucius says, "from being broken."

"He left me."

"I know. A real man admits to his own mistakes."

"At least he's changed for Aly's sake."

"That's right," Lucius says.

"The dark side of chasing the light."

"And through the dark there's light."

"My daughter."

"No matter how dark that tunnel gets."

He embraces her tightly. With one hand on her stomach she kisses him back.

"I'm trusting you blindly," she says.

"No," he says, nudging her chin to look him in the eyes, "you're trusting me fully. Unlike the fool in the deck of Major Arcana. The fool trusts with blind faith costing him his pride."

"What does he have other than his pride?"

"His will. His love. And that makes his heart strong."

"Then he's no fool at all."

"Only if he loves totally and fully with knowledge."

"Then what are we?"

"We are knights who trust the divine light."

"My baby…"

"Beholder of the Goddess. And the Prince. And when we save them, we save us."

"We save all humankind from darkness."

"Yes. It's the way of the warrior. Described in the Prophecy."

"Why my daughter?"

"She's born with the mark of protection. That makes you sacred. Mother of the chosen one."

"What if I fail?"

"You won't. We won't. My father's Coven and their Army won't."

"What's next?" She whispers.

"We train," he says, as Sage lands upon the window, carrion in its talons, "and we feast," he says, "to keep us strong. Like the Hawk, we hunt and we stay fierce," he says, balling one hand into a fist.

"We need you to be strong," she says, her hand to her belly.

"Already?" He stammers.

"Yes." She says. "I'm already late."

"Everything will go as planned," he says, taking one knee. "I promise you," he says, and takes her by the hand. "Let's get married before the baby is born."

"Is that a proposal?" She whispers.

"Will you marry me?" He says, kissing her hand.

"Yes," she says, and they smile, peering into one another's eyes.

The following weeks are rugged as the sun settles into May and the snow melts over the White Mountains. Trainings are rigorous;

they wake at five o'clock AM and begin with movements that mimic the precision of the warrior.

Spring gives way to summer as the heat permeates the landscape. They train with weapons as Hanna becomes ever-more vigil and noticeable.

Their wedding is arranged beneath the cherry blossoms of the neighboring town nestled among the foliage of summer. Jace slits his eyes and jitters nervously in his seat as Hanna's veil is removed and the last of their vows lead to a final kiss. He coughs to suppress his rage - regrettably acknowledging what he thought he could not handle.

Following the wedding vows, conducted by a High Priestess – Reese, who she called upon holding onto the amulet with the thought of Aly and her unborn baby, and of Sterling, who she knew would have presided over them. Reese obliged by coming to the mountains before expected as she's ready to see her own family in the Green Mountains of Vermont.

Bernard feeds Mag-Pie a morsel of a turkey leg from beneath his oversized coat. Gladys and Vienna dine with a goblet of wine, Luther and Archibald are in the company of Diana and Reese who take them on the dance floor; a gold coin is placed in the jar and they take a turn dancing with the bride and groom. In those moments they already feel victorious but in the back of their mind they know of the non-permanence of the moment; but for a minute the *Book of Prophecy* can be put to rest except for Jace who refuses to dance. He leaves the reception with his hands in his pockets and a chip on his shoulder.

And the sisters follow after.

Eleven

Practice commences every morning at five o'clock AM as usual. They begin with Thai Chi then move on to swords and finish with esoteric arts training that encompasses learning mind, body and soul movements. Jace can levitate – suspending his body in the air for a four minute count and Hanna is skilled with the sword; her grace is found in slaying to cut through the blade of the enemy; her skill in defense makes her new father-in-law proud. On this day in June, Hanna and Lucius are awoken from their sleep. Luther, Bernard, Archibald and his wife Diana usher them outside past the clearing and among the rows of prestigious cabins – standing there with their eyes closed they remove their blindfolds to peer at the two-story cedar built log cabin Luther says they can call home.

"A place you can always come back to," Archibald says.

Hanna has tears of both joy and remorse. Lucius hugs his wife, and Jace stands cross-armed down the path with Thor by his side. Sage caws on the roof as if giving her blessing. For the remaining summer all seems well with merely a single mention of the Prophecy. Sydney spoke of enchanting Jace to force him to spill the beans – to force him to come clean with his lies, but Hanna felt all would be revealed in due time; she doesn't want to interfere in his attempt to make amends to his daughter by not trusting him.

The darkness has not made an appearance other than the setting of the sun. Hanna relaxes into her rocking chair on the spacious front porch with her eyes on the athame blade chanting for Sterling to make an appearance, but the blade remains dim and Hanna feels alone.

In the early dawn hours, Reese pays a visit requesting that Hanna take a walk together.

It is June and the dryness permeates the air.

"Summer is beautiful," Reese says, "but the weather hinders the Craft."

"It is dry. And hot," Hanna says.

"Yes, and the veil between the worlds is dense."

"I could not locate Sterling."

"I know love." Reese smiles.

"I want to know how Elusha can side with Goldie."

"We are not sure she has. We only know that she cannot control her desire to seduce which might make her soul dark. That would cause her to be called upon by the darkness."

"So she may not be evil?"

"No. Not all dark souls are evil."

"Why would she steal Clover?"

"Let's hope that it's to send us a message."

"And turn against the dark?"

"Not all things are black and white. Elusha is like a cusp in astrology in that she resides in the fine shade of grey."

"You can say she's on the fence."

"Yes."

"Are there Demons, you know, to fight?"

"The dark can appear demonic. We believe that Goldie may be in charge of the creature. That she may have created him."

"Certainly she is not alone."

"She has some following."

"A demonic Gargoyle."

"Just another totem but one that is so refined by the darkest desires."

"What do they desire?"

"To destroy all that is celestial. The Light."

"Then all would be darkness?"

"Yes. All would be in darkness forever."

"What can you tell me about The Guardian?"

"There is only one Guardian; the Guardian of Light who has two faces; The Goddess of Celestial Light and the Prince of Peace who together make up the Deities of War."

"It sounds complicated."

"All politics are complicated. Even in the astral dimensions."

"My daughter bares the mark of protection."
"She is the vessel that beholds all that is light."
"They have stolen her."
"Being in the possession of the dark makes it vulnerable for the light."
"What's going to happen?"
"A Holy War."
"We are heading toward this war?"
"It's inevitable."
"I've heard that before."
She leads Hanna to the lake where the entire Army and followers are waiting.
"We are here to cleanse our spirits."
Hanna follows Reese to the lake where the Guardians act as High Priestess to the Covens. They wade in the water and bathe in the essence of all that is light. One after another. Gladys and Vienna preside over their soul.
"I cleanse this body of any evil doing," Gladys says.
"And I consecrate this body with ethereal light," Vienna says.
Archibald and Diana guide the followers to the lake and the Hawk caws above as she soars with the spark of light illuminating her by the sun.
"The light is powerful," Bernard says.
"I can feel the eternal in my heart and soul," Archibald says.

"As do I," Diana agrees.

"We all will rejoice in the evening over a feast," Archibald says.

"We will let the eternal good guide us," Luther says.

"We shall brother," Vienna says.

"I attest to the greatness of the light," Gladys attests.

At the feast they dine in the great hall of the recreational center that houses all two hundred guests. They dine with goblets of wine and platters of meats and cheese.

The chiming of fine crystal through the great hall captivates the attention of all guests. Affront rows of tables Archibald stands with the Guardians of the two corners and the Warlock's Coven at his side.

Myself and My Army he begins appearing to have the attention of all *have been in the company of many great witches and warlocks these past months. Together we have trained in techniques that teach us our own strengths while learning our best aspects through Thai Chi movements, military tactics and practices in the esoteric arts. We are not up against a divine entity but persons who abide by the laws of dark forces. The Book of Prophecy has been a guide to most of us who practice witchcraft and Wiccan laws but we must also follow our inner guidance through intuition that we reference as using a third eye. Our enemy is thought to be the Demon of the dark, a dark ruler who seeks power from others and who wishes to have a great following. Recently we lost some followers of the light who went into the dark because he could be seduced by a Guardian whose confusion could be confiscated to use against all that is good. The followers of the light however know that the dark is a fellow opposite – both of which must be in a harmonious balance. Our Divine purpose is to uphold that harmony and to understand the dark while defeating what is evil. All of us shall come together and track the miles to discover our brothers and sisters of the Green Mountains where we will find unity and loyalty from those who know the prophecy as we have come to know it. Let's raise our glasses today to pay respect to the God of War, the Goddess of Celestial Light, the Prince of Peace and the child whose birth signifies unity among the forces of nature – may we come together in peace. May we seek to end evil forever!*

They raise their goblets in protest to the dark and acknowledge the light in each one of them. Lucius exchanges a smile with Hanna who smiles back and Jace raises his glass.

"To brothers," he says as the Warlock's Coven respond the same in return. "To brothers," they say, and Diana holds her goblet high, "To sisters," she says as the followers of Wiccan law raise their goblet in unison. "To sisters," they say in return. They all come together not just as a Pagan Army but as family and friends.

Hanna and Lucius find themselves in the solitude of their own home. A gentle breeze blows through the window and Sage nests by the nearby alpine branches. Her young are growing while Hanna's abdomen appears rounder, fuller, and she can feel her baby's movements. Lucius practices divination over her stomach with an anointed crystal amulet. "It's a boy," he says as the amulet dangles in a clockwise pattern around her naval.
"What will you call him?" She says, sitting up to rest on her elbows to better look into his eyes.
"I've always liked Lucas."
"That's much like Lucius."
"Exactly." He smiles.
"Luther, Lucius and Lucas."
To continue their solitude they head into the clearing where there's a meadow and Hanna can practice sparring. Her movements are swift and graceful as learning Thai Chi has taught her how to be elegant like the feathers

of a bird. Like a peacock piercing the sun with turquoise. She defends her position with a high block, moves in with a roundhouse kick and turns smoothly taking his blade, forcing it from his fingertips. She smiles a wry grin.

"But you will be nine months pregnant," he says, "to be safe we move on to divination."

"But why didn't it save my daughter?"

"We move on to counter curses beyond ointments and enchantments. Fighting fire with fire."

"Then we need the help of the Guardians."

"Yes."

In the ensuing week, Hanna and Lucius maintain their solitude; they become ever more companionable as newlyweds, partners and friends, while Jace feels a disconnect and gravitates toward isolation. In his awkwardness he feels some connection by reading, by thinking about his daughter and by practicing the techniques he has learned at the precipice of the White Mountain. He levitates, suspended in air, feeling the wind course through his body; his stealth in agility stems from being a gymnast but his heart becomes that of a warrior. Of a man. He uses stern concentration to imagine an impending attack and evades smoothly, through leaps and bounds, landing upon a rock and ending in a forward roll. Thor sits perched upon a rock beneath a shady tree and sniffs the air. Jace remains graceful in his presence as if the great wolf can analyze his character.

"We'll be ready, boy," he says, nudging the top of Thor's head who gives a lick in return. "It's the season for the birds and the damn bees," he says, as Thor moves closer and Jace stands, scanning the jutted terrain before him. "But I totally screwed that up," he says, and walks into the distance moving toward the water below.

Lucius and Hanna enter the clearing where the meadow offers scenic wildflowers as Hanna grazes her fingers over the petals.

"He'll be born at the same time as Aly," she says, holding back her remorse.

"We are going to have them both in your arms."

"I want that more than anything."

"I do too, Hanna," he says, swiping the hair from her eyes.

"Jace, I believe, does now as well. I think."

"Yes. We all do. We have a great following and after we track the eighty miles it'll take we'll have another army who will join us."

"For the Fall Equinox."

"It's the right weather by foot. Since so many of us are nomadic we are already trained and equipped for the journey. And when the weather is too cold we always have fire… I'm sure it doesn't matter to give away our location. Those of the darkness are just as familiar with the Prophecy as we are."

"They want us to go there, it seems. The witch calls to me."

"You have all of us to protect you. Never call to them alone."

"I remember."

"Then just follow the Prophecy until you, or we, can intuit another course."

"My mind tells me to keep going."

"For now it's all we can do."

"Sage is in her tree," she points toward the pale blue sky, "she's got her babies in her nest."

"Best she can just be a bird then."

"Yes. As she should be."

"Don't worry," he pats her belly, "we're strong for you and Aly, and we've got Sage there. She'll warn us."

"She's ever-so-vigilant," Hanna agrees.

As the day wanes to night, Thor can be heard howling in the distance among the coyotes. In a quiet embrace on the couch, as they meditate for peace, a tapping at the glass startles their senses.

"Clover!" Hanna exhales.

Followed by a knock on the door.

Hanna opens the door to find Elusha still dressed in a black evening gown.

"I came right away," she says, and barges through the door.

"What is it?" Lucius says.

"I've just escaped. I don't have the time to explain all that I have seen, but what I can tell you is we had not seen a pet – that totem Gargoyle is no animal at all – but a very powerful Demon."

"The same being that killed Sterling?"

"Yes. He is Goldie's master. She is obedient to it."

"What happened to all those men you possessed?"

"I have found that I cannot be so cruel, so evil, but those men I seduced, well, they had a choice – but now I love only one man and we escaped together."

"Escaped from where?"

"Beneath the earth is a grave, or graves, like a giant tomb where they reside. But they like to move frequently. They look for devotees but more importantly …"

"They steal," Lucius pipes in.

"They steal to do what exactly?"

"To make us more afraid," Lucius cuts her off before she can begin a sentence. "But we are ready, if not prepared for the battle against those evil tyrants."

"Did you know that creature was a Demon?"

"I told you what Silver used to teach me… the lore in ancient practices."

"But this is now, today, contemporary, and I need to know the truth."

"I am not here to stay," Elusha musters a word between them. "I have love over evil, and that is most certainly …"

"We understand," Lucius exclaims.

"Love." Hanna says, "They must want evil to rule over love."

"Certainly," Elusha agrees.

"Then love will defeat them," Lucius huffs, placing a hand to Hanna's shoulder.

"Then you have all that you need to know," Elusha says, "I must go by foot. The air is not right for magic."

"Summer is for nature," Lucius says.

"Perfect for making ointments."

"To prepare the magic."

"The Fall Equinox will give way to use magic but until then preparation is all we can do."

And with that message, Elusha makes hast through the door into the warmth of the evening and Hanna sets off to collect all she can to bless, cleanse and consecrate the amulet she wears around her neck. To protect her from evil.

"This crystal is my passage to the light," she says and anoints the crystal in a jar of lavender.

Twelve

Autumn foliage shows its magnificent colors as the forester Bernard leads the following toward Vermont. Crystals graze their necks. Vials of oils adorn their satchels and the scent of eucalyptus permeates the air. The coolness of October subdues the hikers. They stop at the shelters to perch by the fires and dine on their favorite cuisines, and many bring their flasks filled with wine and ale.

"I'm in reverie over spilled blood," Hanna says as the room turns to quiet.
"Not at this time," Lucius says as he eyes Jace and the room grumbles in agreement.
Hanna groans leaving the shelter and into the cool noon and finds Clover atop a street sign. Hanna crosses a small bridge and sees Sage high in the canopy. She is comfortable in their company but she fumbles with the crystal upon her neck and checks the blade in her pocket. Her heart yearns for her daughter and she takes solace on the long trail where she can think and concentrate on all that has transpired. All has moved too quickly, not nearly fast enough. Ahead on the trail she sees Jace staring blankly in her direction.

"How did you get here when you were just there?" She says quizzically.

"I learned to do more than just levitate," he shrugs.

"You can teleport?"

"It's not hard."

"Can you find her?"

"I need your mind for that."

"Elusha said there's graves…"

"Maybe tombs but how can you believe what she says?"

"She made mistakes like you did."

"Nothing like I did," he says, kicking up dust.

"Tell me about spilling blood."

"You know they used to bathe in that shit. Ancient practices spilled a lot of blood."

"Nobody dies in a holy war," a voice says from the distance as they both spin full circle to find Sydney dressed in a full cloak. "No one dies in a holy war," she says again, "there's only a transformation for power."

"The holy war begins after the transformation." Jace adds, "After the following is complete."

"That's a misconception," Sydney interjects.

"I've done my research."

"And so have I."

"It seems that no one can come to an agreement," Hanna huffs.

"The war is for power not death."

"Between good and evil," Hanna agrees.

"To elicit sides."

"That's to prepare for the war," Jace says.

"I've come because we are to prepare for a séance. You can find your cloaks on the bottom floor."

"Since when do cloaks make any difference for doing magic?"

"Since when were you an expert on doing magic?"

"This isn't going to help us get Aly back."

"Then I'll see you at the séance. We are all waiting."

"Thank you Sydney," Hanna musters a smile. Beyond the lush, dense colors of the fall foliage another lone Raven caws overhead.

"That one came here with Thor last night."

"The Ravens have a dark presence here."

"Let's do this séance, I guess."

"They take this very seriously. Just try to get along with Sydney."

"I'll try."

In the basement of the shelter, Jace and Hanna find two cloaks draped over the remaining chair; the men encircle the center table where the women are seated. They promptly pull over their cloaks and Jace takes a stance among the men while Hanna takes a seat at the table. In the darkened room Sydney is seated at the head of the table; she unfolds her hands and they bow their heads.

"We are here to evoke the darkened one," she begins.

"Who put her in charge?" Jace spats, looking furious.

"This is their show," Luther says, slitting his eyes.

"We're looking for the witch and her demon," Lucius says quietly.

In the next few moments the room is quiet as the women begin to hum at the table. Gladys sits at the East with Vienna to the West; Sydney holds the space to the North with Reese to the South. They cover the coordinates to complete the great circle; a pentagram begins to glow, emanating in ethereal light at the center of the table – they first evoke the light they seek to protect them. The pentagram dangles at the center of the table like an illuminated orb. The hum becomes louder like a harmonious tune as the table begins to shake. The women lift their heads and chant *omi-padmi-omi-om* to disturb the spirits of the past. A swirl of light engulfs the room and the pentagram begins to twirl.

"Sterling, are you with us?" Sydney says, and the sound of a baby begins to cry. Hanna stands to her feet lifting her hands to the sound.

"I come to you," a voice whispers in a subtle, sweet sound.

"Who are you?" Hanna says with the light shining around her face and the baby begins to babble, cooing in soft little noises.

"Aly?" Hanna says and the light becomes brighter.

"It's the light from within," Reese says and stands to her feet, bathing her face in the essence.

"The light within her – we have reached it."

"What does this mean?" Hanna says.

"It protects her," Reese explains with her eyes on the pentagram, "we didn't reach the witch or the demon she fosters in her soul but Aly herself."

"The light is our guidance," Sydney says.

"But there must be something else they want," Gladys says.

"Yes," Vienna agrees, "the light protects this little child."

The sisters gather around Sydney.

"If we had known we would have sought to protect Sterling," Amber says.

"If only we had gotten to you sooner," Paisley adds.

"We would have protected you both," Priscilla says.

"I know all of you would have," Hanna says.

"What exactly do you think you could do?" Jace says, stepping forward, "You think you could have saved her?"

"More than you," Amber spats.

"Certainly," Priscilla rolls her eyes.

"Give them a chance," Lucius says,

"We are all in this together," Gladys says.

"Yes we all are." Vienna says, "no matter what could have been done before."

"It's a matter of what can be done now," Reese says.

"Sterling would offer herself to the light," Vienna continues, "she is a High Priestess of the light."

"She is now an overseer of the light." Gladys adds, "Give her a chance to shine."

The sound of a baby laughing startles them.

"What does any of this say about anything?" Jace says, pulling his cloak from his face.

"Jace, Aly is safe," Hanna says.

"No one here could have done anything to stop this," he growls, infuriated.

Lucius steps forward.

"They do not intend to insult your judgment or character."

"They have always been an insult." He glowers, "didn't you ever think that if you hadn't been following me you might have known! Maybe you should have been there – then you could have prevented this shit! You're just as guilty as I am."

"No one has blamed you," Hanna says, "They admitted they would have been there."

"They should have been helping you. Not following me," he says, and storms about the room, tossing the cloak onto the floor.

Luther steps forward alongside Archibald and Bernard.

"We move forward with the Army," he says, and Archibald nods in agreement.

"We need the protection of the light," Sydney says.

"The light is where it should be," Luther says.

"The Goddess of Celestial Light emanates all around her," Reese says.

"We have no choice but to move forward," Luther insists, "but we respect your expertise to evoke the light."

"It has instilled in us great confidence," Bernard says.

"It reaffirms our knowledge," Archibald adds, tapping on Luther's shoulder who nods in return. And the men file out of the room leaving Lucius with the women who also remove their cloaks.

"The Army knows what to do," he says earnestly and he embraces Hanna in a gentle hug as she places her head to his shoulder, wrapping her arms tightly around him.

And the light diminishes.

"The light came through for us," Lucius says entering their private room. "Sydney's intention was to ultimately find the demon, but instead, we found the light through Aly."

"Aly is imprisoned," she says, pacing the room, "and the light is imprisoned within her. I don't know how any of this can be good? How can my daughter be protected while she's in the custody of that demon's witch and the trifling woman who tolerates the death of her own beloved sister?"

"The prophecy holds true. The good will prevail over evil. I'm sure of it."

"I cannot tell you how bad I want my daughter. I want to go straight down under and take my baby back from that filthy creature."

Across the hall in the kitchen the sound of cupboards shutting, opening again, and slamming shut infiltrates the room.

"I'll take a look and see what's going on. You stay here," Lucius says, and enters the hall yielding a sword taken from the den.

"Telekinesis," a voice says from behind as Hanna whirls around to find Jace in the hall.

"Jace," she stammers, taking a step closer, "you're an ethereal body."

"That's right. Like I've said, I've been practicing."

"And telekinesis? Well you're as advanced as Goldie or Sterling was…"

"She used bi-location?"

"The night she took Aly... Sterling said she wasn't for sure."

"I haven't got the skill to protect a physical body yet. She must have taken to Aly right after she got to me."

"Yes. And you were a distraction for the sisters."

"Do you still have the sticks of dynamite?"

"Yes."

"Keep those with you. You never know when you may use them. And meet me at the wooden bridge tonight."

"When?"

"At midnight."

Lucius enters the hall looking perplexed.

"Who are you talking to?"

"Nothing," she says, entering the bedroom and reaching for the covers.

"Nothing?"

"I mean it's no one," she says, yawning.

"I went into the kitchen. Nothing was disturbed."

"Like I said, it's nothing then," she insists, patting the bed for him to join her.

Just before midnight she creeps from bedroom and into the night air; the atmosphere seems opaque and different somehow.

Her bare feet touches the earth in a gentle cool night.

"Jace," she whispers into the night when a flame from a flare sparks the night and in that illumination she sees Sterling's face.

"Hanna, come to us," she says, flickering with the breeze. "You cannot go to them in your condition, as much as you'd like to, but you cannot locate Goldie alone. So Jace goes tonight."

"He's leaving?"

"Goldie acted alone on behalf of the dark side – someone can act alone for the light."

"I can shape shift and possibly enter."

"Enter where?"

"The darkness."

"Where Goldie is in hiding? With our daughter?"

"No. Deeper. Into the dark where the demon stays protected. I'll be able to act from within."

"How will you find them?"

"The laws of synchronicity," Sterling says, "he will follow the path of the warrior and the animal spirits will be his guide."

In the distance a Raven is cawing.

"That's Clover," Sterling says and the light diminishes.

Jace extinguishes the light entirely and moves into the clearing and across the bridge with a whistle for Thor – the amulet still dangles from his neck.

Without a word to Hanna he vanishes into the night and Hanna turns her face to the darkened sky that is engulfed with birds – the ravens hover and move toward the canopy and Sage makes an appearance in the brush. Hanna follows her totem pet to a path into the wooded forest. The Ravens take flight across the stars leaving Clover alone among the branches and she caws while pecking at the ground where the flame had been.

"You didn't say if I should tell anyone," Hanna says to the night making her way along the path. "The Ravens, they must be following Jace," she says again with Sage leading the way. At the end of the path is a house that is illuminated by light; a woman can be seen inside the small cottage removing a tea kettle from the range. Behind her is a wood burning stove that burns kindle.

Sage lands upon the roof and Hanna tip-toes to the front door.

"Come in," the woman says with a warm smile, dressed in purple and accentuated with gold, and places a tea cup for two upon the table. Hanna enters with the screech of the door.

"Have a seat," the woman says, pulling a chair from the table.

"You have met a friend of Sterling's recently," she says, pouring tea from a kettle.

"Yes," Hanna says casually. "Her name is Reese."

"Yes," she agrees, taking a seat from across the table, "she told me you would be visiting here."

She flashes a toothy grin, "My name's Tully, an old mentor for Reese, and she told me about your friend Sterling."

"She was murdered by the demonic beast her very own twin sister decides to follow."

"It is strange in deed to be so dark."

"And so cruel."

"It is a noble thing for Jace to do after taking the dark presence away from the Calvary."

"How do you know?"

"I have a special affinity for being informed of anything that pertains to the prophecy."

"Who are you? I mean, what do you do?"

"I keep to my senses by using psychic energy to unearth anything that does not follow the light. That is how I found Goldie prying in my forests."

"She was here?"

"Not in the flesh. And only momentarily."

"What does she want here with you?"

"Guidance. Power. Knowledge. Anything she can feed the beast."

Hanna sips modestly from her cup.

"Do you see anything in your cup dear?" Tully says with a bitter face.

"Sorry," Hanna says, eyeing her tea cup, "I don't think so."

"Supposed to have two sugar cubes but appears I forgot," Tully says, removing a canister from the cupboard, "Care for some sugar?" She says emphatically, and tosses a cube into her tea cup.

"Thank you," Hanna says.

"You know," Tully becomes serene, "the Druids Army is a modern sect who follow the principles of witchcraft but where you are going there will be Shamans whose knowledge far surpasses the Shakers."

"The Shakers?"

"Spiritual followers who still reside in spiritual squares among the mountains of New Hampshire mostly."

"Then why haven't I met them?"

"They keep to themselves mostly."

"Oh."

"But the Shamans deliver sorcery of medieval value."

"Well, what do you do … you seem to know a lot… I wish Reese had mentioned you."

"The Craft works in mysterious ways," she says, drawing the curtain, revealing a full moon among the stars, "but to answer your question, I am a sensitive or psychic really and my specialty is clairvoyance or remote viewing as it's been called."

"You have precognition or premonitions …
then you knew I was coming… my
daughter… do you know anything…"

"I know much," she insists, removing an
apple pie from the oven, placing it onto the
table, "but we must be cautious of the time…
remote sensing, especially into the
underworld is a careful practice," she says
casually slicing into the pie as Hanna notices
Sage on a branch and all appears still.

Thirteen

Hanna stares at the vortex of a black hole. The smell is rancid; death and decay permeates her senses.

"How are you doing this?" Hanna says holding her nose.

"I just manipulated your energy centers and broke your conscience free of the solar plexus. Don't worry, your body is where it should be. Astral travel is a projection of mind and energy."

There is a pulling sensation upon Hanna's opaque-looking form. She looks at her hands that appear like a fog or a daze in a jet of stream-like smoke. Hanna and Tully waver through the density of the atmosphere while pulling through the stench of darkness. She stares at what seems to be a pool of blood – a curdled quicksand where her heels should be. She feels the sensation of pulling or reaching at her sides as if the dead beckon at her feet. Tully trudges on moving viscerally into the cold and damp dark of the deep. The state of being in Hell surpasses the desolateness of being alone in the dark and pervades her thoughts like a train wreck upon her soul. The underworld delivers its promises of morbid repulsion. Hanna stirs in the mud of it; the atmosphere becomes thicker, denser, and more rancid with each movement. She does not know how anyone could wish to live among the stench. Her daughter being in such a place makes her cringe with grief. She races through time and space with no perception of light. Tully stays firmly at her side ushering her through the dampness. They hover above moving entities that groan with grievances. Hanna thinks she can understand their pain but not their demise to succumb to the bottom of the deepest abyss. Tully advances toward a large gate of cast iron and pries it open unearthing a stench of indescribable proportions and awakening the pits of damnation that reside there.

"This is where grief and sorrow goes when its energy is used for the most heinous of crimes."

"Then that is Goldie," Hanna sneers.

"And Leisha it seems," Tully voices.

"You know of them?"

"Yes. Of course. It's no secret. They are not hiding."

"Then what do you call this place?"

"This is simply the underworld where dreams and desires failed in the hearts of men and women. The reason they became lost souls –

finding themselves in such dire need that they feel they have no other home."

In the distance there's a sound of dogs ravishing the flesh of men. There are screams of terror and the moaning of disease, famine and illness.

"What is all that sound coming from?" Hanna says, shuttering.

"They are spirits or discarnate souls who are bound to their nightmares," Tully says while moving briskly into the open expanse before them like a vast dungeon. They emerge onto a platform of thick turf and Hanna is pulled through another portal. Tully turns to her quickly and pulls on a silver cord Hanna had failed to realize attaches the two of them. She chants a full mantra appearing fully possessed when her face fully materializes and Hanna begins to feel her own hands; they are translucent and lack the natural color of beige. She finds herself standing on the platform to a large bridge that merges the landscapes that are jutted with protruding rock formations over rough terrain. There are more sounds like distant storms and groans of cats. Hanna cannot distinguish past and present as if time had long stood still. She winces at the emergence of a ghostly image that appears with only eyes and a torso. She quivers and is startled by the colony of

Ravens that flock overhead and land sporadically all around them. A Raven pulls at a substance from the ground like the mangled remains of a large earthworm and croaks in a loud shrill sending the rest back to flight. Hanna stifles all questions and watches the torso morph into the grim creature with piercing flame-red eyes as it begins to snarl and ravage at her feet causing her to step backward and Tully lights a flame out of thin air using psychokinetic energy to drive the beast into the dark by the light of the flame.

"The darkness does not like the light no matter what form it takes."

The beast morphs again standing erect with bony hands that shields its face from the flame.

"Keep moving," Tully says, ushering Hanna over glass-like pebbles that splinter beneath her feet. She glimpses at a green amulet wedged between her toes on terrain full of lava rock. She pulls at the amulet, still connected to a chain collar, and rubs her thumb over its smooth surface revealing the eye of the massive cat. As she presses further with both hands on the totem the cat emerges bearing its fanged teeth and startling the Ravens evermore that flock into the shadows. Tully sways with hips that move to and fro as she waves them onward motioning to the deep and ever-darkening vortex through Hell. "The beasts might be shape shifting but we're not fools who don't have magic up our sleeves," she says with the stealth of the magnificent Jaguar looking regal in the position of a predator. The Ravens are held at bay among the shadows and the beasts that fill dreams with night terrors can be heard in low monotonous groaning and the screeching of nails in the dirt like steak knives across a dinner plate are forging among them. Before them in their sights are large formations of lava rock that are distinct with the bodies of fallen men and women buried in ash among them. Tully stops subtly to contain her breath. "To defeat your enemy, you have to first know your enemy."

Hanna's instincts have her grabbing at her abdomen thinking about the baby within. Thinking too about the baby she has lost.

"The beast that killed Sterling…"

"No beast such as these," Tully says, crouching in a low position and Hanna follows suit, "but the demons of inner turmoil like the death and decay of a rotting hell and peering over the corner of the precipice Hanna kinks her neck stretching her body forward right into the breath of a gaunt face and tarnished teeth with slits where eyes should be; staring into it is the deepest of dark spaces where one would pass into the abyss and be eternally lost in the confines of despair.

Hanna's face drops as she loses her breath and Thor leaps from the dark edges of Hell's door and breaks her trance; Jace approaches looking merely like exoskeleton being internally dark.

"You have seen," he says, "now leave!"

He forces a light to her eyes – a blinding, seemingly enigmatic light with Tully's voice falling in the distance, "I don't think she knows what she has done," she says, waving as if saying goodbye.

"Who?" Hanna calls back, with the retreating of the cat.

"Goldie of course," she says and Hanna's body forces upright from the bed. She pants heavily, touching her neck and trembles with night sweats.

"What is it Hanna?" Lucius says, sitting up from the bed and turns the light on. Hanna glares at the clock, only minutes have passed since she stepped into bed.

"Minutes?" She says, looking wildly finding her room and all around her as she remembers it.

"But I've been gone for hours," she exclaims, bewildered.

"Gone? Gone where?"

"Tully took me to where they reside. To a very dark underworld where…"

"Tully?" Lucius says, sitting up from his position, looking even more perplexed.

"Tully McDermott?"

"I didn't get her last name," she says softly.

"She's one of the most brilliant witches that lived."

"That lived? As in no longer living?"

"No. Tully died several years back."

"Tully told me Reese said I would be visiting her."

Hanna leaps from the bed and turns abruptly to the sound of the window and finds Clover with the green amulet hooked to a chain collar within its beak.

Hanna knocks on the door with vigorous attention. Reese answers, wearing her satin bath robe, with Hanna dangling the amulet inches from her face.

"Hanna," she says, startled, "it's awful late, is everything alright?"

"Do you know what this is?" She says, ushering herself past the door.

"No, I'm not sure," Reese admits.

"This belongs to Thor… do you know where I was tonight?"

"No, I haven't a clue."

"You told Tully I'd be seeing her. Paying her a visit."

"Tully?" She says, pausing to take a breath. "Please sit down. You have to tell me what has happened?"

For the next half hour Hanna fills Reese's attention with details of the harrowing depths of the demonic underworld. Reese braces herself into the chair and lets out a sigh.

"She didn't want to alarm you," she begins, "but you had an out-of-body experience and not only that," she adds, "but you have experienced time travel."

"Time travel?"

"Yes. In the astral dimension time and space breaks down where there is no past, present or future. But time stands still as if everything is happening now."

"So I saw Tully when she was alive?"

"The cosmos doesn't apply the same laws of time so in a sense yes. Tully was superbly psychic and a highly evolved witch."

"But I walked through the woods along a trail, and I came to her house…"

"And you were out-of-body, and you were traveling where time breaks down and does not exist."

"What about Jace? Thor?"

"Imagine he thinks he can enter the darkness and see the light."

"It's the most terrifying and dreadful existence."

"Those beasts in the depths of darkness live in anguish and languish in their own misery while subjugating others to the same fate."
In the next hour Hanna takes leave and returns to Lucius to finally get some useful sleep. At noon the next day she is awoken by a knock at the door.

"The trail is much overgrown," Hanna says as she walks her earlier path alongside Sydney and the Sister's Coven. "The amulet had its use I assume," Sydney says, "and found its way back."
"That must mean something," Amber says, with her head down, stepping over fallen limbs. They stop at the end of the path where the trees are too overgrown and the house before them is cloaked in vines and ivy.
"Is that the house you say you entered?" Priscilla asks.
"Yes." Hanna looks sullen, "She was inside, making a pie, and she poured us tea."
"I've never experienced a time warp," Paisley says with a sigh.
"Well, we are your welcoming committee," Paisley pipes in, bouncing slightly on her toes.
"That's right sisters," Sydney agrees. "We are here to welcome you back to earth."

Hanna takes one last look at the deserted home she had just ventured and finds Sage nestled onto the roof plucking at its meal; she realizes any sign of Sage is a clear indication that the dark must not be near and without the sight of Clover anywhere near.

Back at the shelters Hanna steps into the well-lit cabin that's hidden by colorful foliage along the Long Trail. She walks down the stairs into an open room with tables and a cafeteria that has been decorated in blue.

"This is your party," Sydney says.

"Your baby shower," Amber smiles.

Hanna's eyes dazzle upon the chandelier above a table that is illuminated with four candles that represent the four corners and Sterling's image flickers upon the wall.

"Welcome Hanna," she says, smiling radiantly, shining in a flowing robe like a tunic.

"I knew you would want her to be here with us," Gladys says, extending her arms. She takes Hanna to a seat that has been arranged by a lightly burning fire and places a ribbon around her shoulders. The Guardians, The Sister's Coven, Diane, Reese and the female followers each brought a pot luck dish. They feast over stew, meats glazed in honey, casserole dishes and fresh baked desserts. They play music over an old piano and play games. Hanna opens her gifts finding hand-quilted blankets, scarves, and gloves.

Vienna breaks open a vile of blessed oils. The Sisters and The Guardians guide Hanna to a table where she lays on her back. With her abdomen exposed they begin to sing in a harmony like a lullaby with Reese chanting "Bless this child Divine Mother."

"On this day," Gladys calls, "we ask the spirits of the birth mother to guide this child and his mother on their journey."

"The power of the most ancient spell must be anointed over the mother of the chosen one," Vienna says.

"Elders of the Divine Light," Gladys says, removing a lid from the vile, "we call upon your guidance and intuition to make divination succeed at all times for the New Mother."

"May we bless this mother to find her daughter," Sydney adds, and removes another vile from the table; she pours warm, soothing liquid onto her stomach and they all begin to chant in unison. The light of Sterling glows brighter, reflecting from the candles that burn with the scent of spice.

"The Elders of the forest. Of the Earth Plane. Of the Celestial Realm and the Mountains have heard you," Sterling says in a voice as sweet as a bell.

Hanna feels the kicks and tumbling of her son within her abdomen as her eyes roll slightly and she becomes conscious of another realm – she leaves the room in an extension of her physical body again.

"This is the astral plane," Sterling says standing before her in long flowing robes. "The Elders called upon me before Goldie did the work of the darkness. It was time that I join them as I had done my services in the physical realm. Here, myself and the Elders can assist you and the following on your journey."

In the mist of golden light Tully emerges in full form, looking physical but also translucent and shimmering with Divine Light.

"I was with you in the outer realm of the underworld, and now you are here in the realm of Celestial Light. Having seen both you can make your choice of your own free will to continue following the path of the light.

"I would never choose any other way."

"We have enchanted your son with the spell of Celestial gifts. He will be ever protected."

"And my daughter?"

"The dark prevailed against the light. Not because we are blind and cannot see through the dark but because the dark has advanced beyond sorrow. Beyond fear. And into the most cruelest evil."

"They shall fool us no more," a voice says as the most enigmatic Wizard appears standing before Hanna. His staff made of seemingly pure gold is as tall as he is and his robes flow in luminescence, wrapped around his body and flowing in layers as if the wind were blowing through feathers.

"We have given to you the gift of the light in the body of the Goddess," he says, and waves his staff – casting a cloud-like aura in front view.

"She is with your daughter now," Sterling says.

There, before Hanna's eyes is Goldie doing the work of the dark. And the witch stirring blood with tarnished fingers over runes she uses to predict a future for the child she holds in her grizzly protection.

"Where is she? Where are they?" Hanna groans.

"It's not a matter of where now but a matter of where they are going and the journey that takes them there." The Elder says with a smile that is radiant by high cheekbones and appearing optimistic despite the circumstances.

Hanna suddenly hears the sound of music as if the voices of Celestial Radiance embodies the richness of fine China and the chiming of bells. Then, she lies awake with her abdomen fully anointed in eucalyptus and spearmint spices - penetrating its therapeutic aroma to her son who she feels kicking from within.

"Welcome back again," Sydney says, and the women gather around her. Hanna stands from where she is and begins to waltz about the room.

"I heard the most beautiful music," she says, drawing the curtain away and finding Sage nestled among the branches in the trees.

"The Elders have called upon you," Reese explains.

"Tully was there. And Sterling."

"They must have joined the Council of Elders," Gladys says.

"That must be, sister," Vienna agrees, removing a small charm from her bracelet. "This is also a charm of protection," she says, swaying the pendant that is in the form of two sides of a heart, "one for your daughter and the other for your son," she says, placing the pendant on the necklace with the amulet.

"Thank you," Hanna says, turning her gaze back to Sage, "do you go and visit her?" She whispers out the window, from within as Sage wrestles among the branches and glides into the air, circling overhead like a winged warrior.

In the twilight hours of the following morning Hanna reflects on her experiences and imagines that her journey has just begun. "Jace learned to levitate," she says, casting her eyes to the horizon, "why can't I at least leave my body at will?"

Lucius sinks his teeth into a ripe, red apple and chucks the rind over the edge of the precipice.

"I cannot speak for him," Lucius says, "but all I know is he had been practicing real hard and saving his energy."

"For what purpose?"

"I suppose only he knows that answer."

Hanna and Lucius are startled when Luther enters the trail, "We are to leave tomorrow," he says, with a nod, and Lucius renders a mock solute.

"Very well," Luther gives a slanted grin, "carry on," he says and makes his way into the forest followed by Bernard and Archibald who yield muskets over their shoulder.

"Preparing to have a night's meal," Lucius explains and takes Hanna by the hand, "Don't worry," he says, "many witches and warlocks have yet to levitate." And he kisses her upon the hand, making her smile.

Candace Meredith

Fourteen

They reach the Northern-most summit of Pico Peak using the rough and rugged terrain of the Long Trail in the weeks that pass with the waxing and waning of the moon. With the break of a small branch that has lost its leaves the once still wild starts stirring.

"Been awaiting your arrival," a masculine voice says from behind as Luther, Archibald, Bernard and Lucius turn full circle. They hear the faint chuckling of a woman as the pair exit the tree line and onto the path that led them there.

"I'm Herman," the man says with a shorter physique and tousled dirty blond hair, "and this is my wife Eva." The entire following removes heavy, burdening packs from their back at Luther's gesture for all to take a break.

"How is it you know of our coming?" Luther smiles, "you have a psychic among you?"

"We're all psychic in these woods," the man smiles.

"Then our party shall fit right in," Bernard gestures to the group.

"We have read your sermon in the paper," Eva says, with a slightly parted smile, and long locks that remind Hanna of Sterling, making her turn when Eva waves to the crowd aside her.

"May you all follow us back to the lodging," Eva says.

The lodges are fit for a resort; many of them being second homes, the Shamanic parties prefer to travel often and have come to call home the lodge where they reside at any given time. Luther realizes how fortunate he is that the Shamans are presently in their quarters in Vermont and thanks Chris the news reporter under a faint breath that extends to the outer region.

"I need to introduce you to my wife Diane," Archibald insists and extends his hand toward her.

"Sister," Eva says, with a radiant smile.

"Likewise sister," Diane says and they embrace in warm gratitude.

From the back window Diane can see the expanse of the Green Mountains and, like New Hampshire, there are cottages that span the horizon.

"There have been shadows among us," Eva says lightly muffled.

"I have seen them or one," Hanna says.

"All the energies converged over Aly," Lucius says, placing his arm around her.

"Aly?" Eva says.

"My daughter," Hanna explains.

"The child who has been stolen," Lucius says.

"Yes, I see," Eva nods.

"The reason we have come here," Luther says. "To make an alliance among the Shamans," Luther admits.

"But first," Archibald insists, "let us enjoy some company…"

"Over tea," Eva says.

"And some ale, dear," Herman grumbles.

The entire village hosts the followers and together the following encompasses over four hundred practitioners of fable and lore.

Upon a knock on the door, Eva scurries toward the door, before opening, she waves with the brush of a hand, "It's just Tibal," she says, giggling a little, "clairsentience," she says, "I could sense him coming a mile away."

"Someone missing a three-legged cat?" He says, darting his thumb as Eva ushers him to come inside.

"We have guests," she says.

"I noticed," Tibal says, "the village suddenly got more popular," he says, "what do we owe this company?"

"Don't you read the paper?" Herman says, his hand upon his shoulder.

"No," Tibal admits firmly, "I haven't read that thing in years. Always full of problems."

"Well this may be one of the biggest," Herman says, looking grim.

"I might take a seat then," Tibal says, walking slightly hunched and aged.

Calmly he takes a seat at the table and begins, "I've come here to inquire if anyone is aware of the black stallion that wondered into the village?"

The Wiccans turn to one another quizzically, "What stallion has come to the village?" Eva asks.

"A fine black horse with a white chest, and white between the eyes, still wearing a saddle … but with no rider among it."

Everyone stands quiet. "That horse carried with it a letter between its teeth that Drake removed very carefully then that horse took off into the forest and just simply vanished."

"So the question is… who killed the messenger?" Herman says, and Eva slits her eyes.

"What did the note say?" Eva ponders as he begins to speak and the men in the room grumble when a thick, dense fog-like swirl of smoke infiltrates the room and standing before them are two women dressed in velvet-like black dresses and black, heavy boots that clank against the wooden floor as they waltz about the room.

"Goldie!" Hanna gasps.

"And her protégé," Vienna huffs.

"How can you come here?" Gladys bellows, and Luther removes a small sword from his scabbard and charges in full angst, but Goldie merely huffs as the ring of smoke becomes thicker and like a force field Luther is thrown backwards as his sword clanks against the wall.

"It's just a force field of bad energy," Lucius sneers.

Goldie sniggers.

"Bad energy?" Leisha says, curling her lip, "I still prefer avant garde."

Goldie croaks more loudly like a squealing chicken.

"You're both just pure evil," Hanna says, tucking away her abdomen behind Lucius.

"Maybe so sister," Leisha says, "but our place is as High Priestess to the Prince of Darkness. He is our ruler and he is the path to power and splendid fortune."

"No fortune should be great enough as to kill a most beloved sister. A true blood relation," Luther says.

"My sister would have chosen her own fate just as I have," Goldie says.

"Yes, sister," Leisha agrees, her smile broadening, "just as we have received a new recruit…"

"That's right," Goldie grins, "we have some fresh blood on our coat tails, now don't we…"

Hanna rushes both women, as to grab their necks, when the smoke becomes so thick she cannot be seen and they dissipate, leaving the room with an aroma of rot and decay.

"Why are they coming here?" Hanna says, with clenched fists and tightness in her face.

"Company loves misery," Lucius sniggers.

"In a way you are right," Tibal says, with a hoarse breath, "they seek the company of the misfortunate who very often had no other choice."

"The dark brought with it a menacing aura," Gladys sniffles.

Tibal coughs, choked up, and begins to speak until Luther and Archibald catch his fall.

"That smoke is toxic," Vienna says.

"Hurry," Eva says, "get everyone outside."

They carry Tibal to a well-lit front porch and Hanna casts her eyes toward Clover – cawing in darkness.

"Something else is amiss," Hanna says but soon discovers Sage flanked on the opposing side of the forest when a lone black horse walks into view. Hanna steps off the balcony and onto the cool, damp earth, slowly and deliberately, she approaches the animal and Sage soars to a nearby branch, tufting up her wings.

"Careful my love," Lucius says, and he speeds his pace to catch up with her.

"I don't know how but my intuition tells me this horse was sent by Jace."

Tibal's breath is labored, "The letter," he croaks, before passing out cold.

"We will have to take him to the healer – a Shaman by the name of Java," Herman says.

"Hanna, can you use your mind, your intuition, to read the letter?" Lucius says.

"The letter says something about a book," Sydney says, stepping into view among her coven who teleport with grace.

"I can't see anything," Hanna says.

"The letter is shrouded in darkness," Sydney explains, "and so are the contents of the book."

"The Book of Prophecy?" Hanna asks.

"But we have been over that book a dozen times," Lucius says.

"I don't think it's the same book. It appears to be another book with hidden information."

"The air they came in on was toxic," Amber says, slitting her eyes upon the horse.

"Maybe Jace was on that horse," Priscilla says.

"We can't merely speculate," Luther says, "but someone must have come on this horse and that smoke was certainly vile in nature."

"A compliment from the Guardian I suppose," Paisley says.

"Yes, sisters," Sydney agrees, "her smoldering cauldron would certainly contaminate us all."

"Why is Tibal being the only one affected?" Amber asks.

"Because he saw the letter," Sydney muses.

"He and the messenger were the only ones to see its contents?" Hanna muffles.

"Drake would not have read its contents without seeing an elder in the village," Herman explains.

"Stay alert," Luther says, taking a limp Tibal into his barren arms.

"We have promised Hanna that we are ever more vigilant," Sydney says.

"That is gracious of you all," Gladys agrees.

Hanna places her palm upon the horse's muzzle and he steps graciously toward her; their energies collide and she feels an inner connection with his spirit.

Hanna inserts one foot into the reign and hoists herself onto the horse looking regal and prominent with a fully round abdomen.

"I will call you countess," Lucius says.

"And you are my count as well," she leans forward as the horse bows with its front legs tucked beneath him and Hanna looks up while patting his mane, and notices the North Star in front view.

"The North," she says, "do you suppose this is Leisha's horse?"

"I don't believe so," Luther says, "remember to trust your instincts. Your intuition is more keen than logic."

Behind them the night is gleaming by the fullness of the moon.

The following morning a congregation meets in the expanse of the outdoors, forming a circle, with the mountains surrounding them.

"The Shamans here are so beautiful," Hanna says, "they have the appearance of aboriginals."

"Yes," Lucius agrees, "like our North American tribes."

One of them, an aged warrior, stands amid the great circle of hundreds, wearing only tribal head gear over long, gray hair and arm bands of black.

The aged Shamanic warrior points a staff made of bone, toward Hanna, and then the sky above them.

"They recognize you as their Heir to the path of light," Luther explains, and offers her a hand as she joins the warrior at the center of the circle. She bows as she has become accustomed by her practices in Thai Chi and the Chief Warrior nods in return.

He waves his staff again and the drumming begins.

"This is the Shaman welcoming party," Luther says to Lucius and the great parameters of the Green Mountains. Men in great ceremonial attire hammer their drums and chant with voices. "Great Wind" is the name of the elder who commences the ceremony, and known as Raul to the tribes' people.

Matthew, Bill and Ned of the Warlock's Coven begin to dance to the humming of the wind instruments.

"We are to join in on this ceremony through dance to evoke the spirits who will guide us on this journey," Luther says.

Archibald raises a sword and the Druids' Army draw their weapons, sparring against one another in a mock battle; in the center is Hanna, encircled by a dance that is surrounded by a battalion of strong forces – all coming together to fight the darkness of insipid hell.

The drumming, the dance, the practice of the arts, lasts for hours; then they feast. They thank the outer realms for the food on their tables and raise their goblets, filled with sweet red wine, to one another for coming together on a journey – anticipating the course ahead knowing the dark is stirring in the shadows to spread terror among the people – to recruit them into evil and spread the intrepid malice like a terrible disease on the men who know the dark side of chasing the light; they therefore must be prepared to protect the light at any cost.

The Guardians, The Sister's Coven, The Warlocks, The Druid's Army and the Shamans are a force of over four hundred men and women who follow the Craft of the esoteric arts through evocation of the outer worlds, of divination and above all – the oneness of celestial light that oversees them. They have prepared for battle in order to fight through the dark and to make free the Goddess of Celestial Light and the Prince of Peace.

With the drinking of wine and feasting they prepare their bodies for the impending war that is prevalent within the Book of Prophecy. In the following morning they prepare their bodies and their minds for the march to the summit of Mount Katadhin – to the Northern-most peak when the veil between the worlds grows thin and hell has reached earth.

Hanna searches for Sage and Clover to no avail. She mounts her black stallion of a horse thankful to be off her feet with the birth of her baby pending so soon and rides among the army of practitioners toward the rising sun and further toward the North.

Back at the Shamanic village, Tibal heals by the side of Java, the natural healer, who uses medicinal herbs and hot chamomile tea to nurture his weary body. Java is a lean woman who has practiced the arts of witchcraft since she learned she could foresee traumatic events before they occur. She took upon practicing medicine to heal others who follow the light that she sees in her mind's eye as being the haven for departed entities. She sees her own mother in the light of fire the way Hanna calls upon Sterling. She knows the darkness is thick and heavy among them.

She fears the worst is yet to come – but to what extent she is uncertain. The demon, she feels, is strong, proud and hungry to be the ruler of the kingdoms – not just the underworld but over and above all that is sacred. He is among them in greed and holds over the souls in his grasp in anguish, encapsulating them in the only form their souls know – if only they could set them free – they might succeed in this war that presides over them.

"The impending deaths," she says over Tibal, "is grave," she continues… "I fear for our fellow Shamans…"

Tibal parts his eyes ever-so slightly and chokes, "The following," he tries to find his breath…

"Rest easy," Java says, "do not speak," and she places stones to his chest – the points of the chakra centers where she intends to open his energy centers that had been blocked by toxins brought on by the dark followers.

And the entire Calvary begins its journey forward to the summit. To the North. And Hanna can see the North Star still lit by twilight.

Candace Meredith

Fifteen

The hike to the summit of Mount Katahdin was treacherous. Luther, Archibald, Bernard and Herman found Percival, the Shaman sorcerer, to be a tough guide whose age did not slow his maneuverability. Percival, who they call Percy, took the place of Tibal as guide. Percy is all brawn who produces timber for the Shamanic tribes of Vermont. He points to an ever-darkening sky. The landscape appears barren and unproductive; a lone abandoned house sits seemingly undisturbed upon the great mountain. A shutter breaks free and crashes to the ground. The air is cold as October gave way to winter; they know they will need shelter. Hanna turns her attention to a bird fluttering in the thick of low-lying branches and retrieves Clover in her clutch; she has a broken wing. Hanna searches the sky for Sage but she is nowhere in sight. The clouds move to cover the sun creating an omnipresent gray over the landscape. Percy begins to chant creating a mood of calm in the quiet and stillness before them. A single Raven lands upon a bare twig – glaring. Then another flutters by landing in an opposite tree. Luther and Archibald draw their swords and another Raven swoops in among them while a large flock of Ravens begin to cover the sky turning the glint of sunlight to dark. Hanna mounts her horse who is stirring in low grunts of trepidation. Beneath the gray covered sky the jutted landscape begins to break apart with a searing bolt of lightning. A crack in the earth's surface splits from the peak of Mount Katadhin as the face of the Goddess slits her eyes and she morphs from the clouds appearing purely medieval in a velvet green dress with gold trim; her green eyes pierce through the dismal, bleak weather in sheer force and power. She raises both hands over sleek black hair crowned in black roses and forces another strike of lightning, parting the landscape and illuminating the sky as the Ravens begin to stir.

"I am called upon to test you – ever vigilant ones," she says with a mighty voice.
The Ravens claw at the backs of the Druid's Army who draw great swords and shield their faces dressed in suits of armor. From the jutted opening of the terrain horses emerge from beneath; skinny, disheveled faces breathe heavily in the angst of the nightmare.
"They have released hell upon us," Bernard says.

The horses are drawn by barren men of mere shadows.

"How do you kill what's already dead?" Luther calls.

"You survive," Archibald says and the massive army becomes consumed by the ravishing claws of birds and the stampede of the horses; the shadows draw great staffs with the sharp blade of an axe. In the scuttle of military-style fighting the Druids do not hesitate. Lucius leaps a significant bound as the axe of the dead army braises his shins; the horrid sounds of men falling into the cliffs alarm Hanna and she calls upon the magnificent cat from the amulet upon her neck. The great cat leaps into action pointing its face to the ground below; he uses the force of a massive paw, clearing its path. The underworld splits into a cavernous canyon, concave as the catacombs. Lucius strikes one horse centered to its pointed muzzle; the blade, anointed with oil, forces the beast and its master into tiny particles of dust; "The anointment," he hollers, "it's working."

"Like Holy water," Bernard says.

"We pagans never undermine your expertise good sir," Lucius says.

"And I onto yours," Bernard says, drawing his own sword and slashing at a swift Raven landing it onto the ground and it turns immediately to dust.

"Ashes to ashes," Bernard says.

The Sister's Coven huddle in a circle back-to-back creating a unified aura of protection as a light sphere of energy can be seen surrounding them; the Ravens cannot penetrate. Hanna holds Clover – her broken wing laying limp at her side – and joins the Shamans in a chant but the great mountain begins to crumble beneath them; with the slash of the axe blade men become shadows of the night – imprisoned in their own minds by the darkness. Archibald runs in a speed of uncanny proportions, drawing his blade, as the open space gives way entirely and Jace draws a knight's sword, blocking his axe from penetrating the horses drawn by shadows.

"Jace," Hanna calls forcefully, "No! Please! You have lost your way."

And he turns to her, raising his fist, slamming the blade into the earth, splitting the mountain entirely that gives way beneath them and the Goddess of Storms vanishes. Echoing all around them is a horrid cackle of a woman – and of Goldie – as one by one the army and its followers become shadows and there is no more light from the sun. All is black. The Ravens are cawing. The underworld opens like a expansive womb – drawing them in and downward; the sounds of men falling, the Ravens cawing, the chanting and cackling is cacophonous. The four sisters are unscathed; Lucius is growing exhausted; Luther, Archibald and Bernard fight steadily – turning the dark army to dust; the dark army turning men to mere shadows. The mound of earth that is mountainous gives way and crumbles entirely as a ship, made of the Dead Sea, passes before the clouds, the shadows and their horses flock to it like a welcoming ceremony and the pagans fall into the catacombs with no chance of the light around them – enclosing the survivors within mounds of mud.

"They've sent us to hell," Bernard screams in terror and agony as his leg suffers fractures from the descent.

"This isn't hell," Hanna says, digging into her cargo pockets, lighting a flare, "I've been to Hell, the underworld, and it's far more rancid."

"This is like a tomb," Luther says.

"They've sent us to our graves," Archibald agrees, "there's only about fifty of us remaining."

"My horse, look at him," Hanna says, peering at the bones that protrude from flesh.

"You will have your totem pet as guide," Sydney says.

"Yes, keep Rajah with you," Amber agrees.

"Can you teleport us out of here?" Bernard says.

"It doesn't appear so," Sydney explains, "this place is a low level energy field."

"Bad energy," Priscilla says.

"Yes sisters. The energy field here makes it too difficult to locate a vortex or an energy center for teleportation."

"The Shamans are trying to generate an energy field but to no avail," Hanna says.

"It's stagnant," Luther adds, "no warlock can find a vortex either."

"We will have to climb our way out," Matthew, of the Warlock's Coven says.

"The mud and clay from the mountain appears too dense," Marcus says.

"But we still have our swords," Archibald says with slight optimism.

"Down here, they appear not to be much good to us," Grant says, spitting to the earth, frustrated.

"What are we to do without food?" Bill says, "and for how long?"

"How about that cat," one of the followers says, appearing disgruntled.

"Touch my cat," Bernard says, "and you'll lose both hands," he sneers.

"Stop!" Gladys says, looking sooty, but untouched by demonic followers, "this is exactly what darkness will do to us…"

"We have to keep our wits about us," Vienna agrees.

"Or we succumb to sorrow and despair," Sydney says.

"I still have a canteen," Ed says, "I haven't lost my pack."

"I have flares and sticks of dynamite," Hanna says.

"But all the walls, the top soil above us, could cave in upon us," Lucius says.

"And I still have the athame," she says, "Sterling may have the answers."

"The energy here is just too low for the work of sorcery," Sydney reiterates.

"Which just might be the plan of darkness," Bernard growls.

Together they form a circle taking out the only possessions they have; some have canteens and others have freeze dried foods in packs; from the flame of the flare they have an hour of light.

"They can make us hungry but they cannot devour our soul," Archibald says, and Herman with Percy begin to sing in a low monotone hum, listening for any sign of an opening – a way out of the dark of the desolate catacombs.

Winter settles upon them; soon, more snow will blanket the ground above them. They have only dynamite among them now. They sit in imminent darkness using sound to keep them from delirium. A month passes and their canteens are empty. They pass along the parcels of freeze dried food they have among them when they hear a stir from above; the ground shakes loose some dirt and debris of rocks that fall among them. In a slit of gravel moved away from a large boulder the ground gives way and a voice that is aged and coarse calls, "Watch out below! The boulder will fall through!" They feel the sides of the hollow tomb and huddle against the far edge of rock when the boulder breaks loose and the rubble atop the boulder creates an opening that is hard to see due to the thickness of gray clouds that blocks the sun. Archibald, Luther and Bernard lead the fifty survivors toward the opening, hoisting them upward one at a time until each reaches the surface of a barren landscape – full of bone from the bodies that turned to Shadows. The daylight is not permissible and now the groaning of souls can be heard through the land.

"Tibal," Herman says.

"Java," Eva says, and they embrace.

Diane approaches and extends her hand to both women but says nothing because her eyes say it all.

Hanna drops her face, feeling sullen, and scoops up bones of a lone bird with a broken wing.

"Clover," she says, and her eyes begin to water.

"My totem does not work in these conditions," Sydney says, rubbing her amulet.

"I am no closer to my daughter," Hanna says forcefully.

"Wait," Tibal utters a breath as his legs buckle beneath him and he collapses with his head resting on the lap of Java. "You didn't get the letter," he muffles and extends his hand to her with the crumpled bit of paper looking tarnished in his fingers. Hanna picks up the letter, unfolds it, and reads the print of a well-wrought hand: *Spilled Blood in the Name of True Love.*

"Jace must have written this," she says and folds the paper, putting the pieces into her pocket aside the dynamite she never used — afraid to collapse the walls around them.

"I have lost my daughter. Sterling. Clover. And my heart bleeds."

"I do not understand the meaning of all this," Bernard says, tucking away the three-legged cat. "How defeat can turn Pagans to shadows. Wouldn't they have to perform an evil deed to be turned or converted to evil? How can a man who fights for the light be transformed?"

"They repress the light in their soul by locating their fears and their sorrows," Sydney says.

"Like she said before," Amber says, "no one dies in a Holy War."

"They just transform," Priscilla says and Paisley nods.

"I am lost now," Hanna breathes, "and I no longer have Jace."

"We all have each other," Lucius says, and turns his cheek as Tibal takes his last breath and Java closes her eyes with tears streaking down her face.

"The great epic battle…" Bernard says.

"Not all is lost," Luther says, "but we need to carry this man home for a proper burial."

They leave the sunken land that used to be a great mountain of the Goddess of Storms and traverse their steps – the weather is so cold the body is well preserved as they take turns carrying Tibal's lifeless body home.

Hanna stretches her neck to the sky finding only the face of the Goddess who rules the weather – and no sign of Sage, but the Goddess parts her lips and blows the winds over the land – wrecking havoc where they stand thus forcing them onward.

"Is the Goddess of Storms evil magic?" Hanna asks as she gazes at her face until she retreats into the clouds and all that is left is a smoke colored sky.

"The Goddess ruled the greatest mountain – in that way she has been defeated too," Sydney explains. "She is neither good nor evil but only controls what was the highest mountain."

"I don't understand this need for harsh weather," Hanna objects.

"Understanding the weather is like understanding a war," Luther says.

"Or how a woman can kill her own sister," Lucius adds.

Hanna becomes exhausted. And there is frost with each step. She is due in weeks and is relieved to be back at the Shaman's land after a few stops along the trail at the shelters. But Herman drops to his knees – seeing that his land and his people's houses have been burned. The naked atmosphere makes them quiver and his people, the survivors, step out of the brush to stay warm and dry. Some of them have already erected temporary shelters but their animal pens have been opened and only a few of them astray. Odell, the farmer, greets Herman and Eva along with Percival and their guests then places a hand over his friend.

"Thank you for bringing him to us... I am sorry now that we all could not join in the great battle of the dark but the dark has defeated us still."

"Not all could go," Java intervenes, "our people are not all fighters – we are Shamans and we look for guidance from the Spirits of our ancestors – some of us had profound revelations not to go."

"And you were right," Archibald says, "you may not have houses – but you have each other. Had you gone your soul may have been stolen by the forces of the dark army."

"There are so few of you left," a dark skin Shaman woman says, named Kiana.

"Yes, the dark army has claimed most of the following."

In the light of morning a dismal speck of light glints from the snow.

"What is the source of that light?" Hanna says and she begins to dig deeply into the snow – there, she finds Sage covered by a fallen branch. "Just in the nick of time," she says and removes the branch from the magnificent talons of the beautiful bird of prey. Sage belts out a caw and flutters her wings – standing large and proud from the shoulder of its sorcerer. Hanna pats the bird's soft feathers feeling an ounce of relief when the assembly unites to burn the body of their dear friend in order to allow the smoke to carry his soul upward – toward the everlasting home.

Upon a stone they chisel: *Tibal Williams "Ancient Bear"*

And erect a totem pole, much like Sterling's but without a divination orb – instead, they carve the face of brother bear whose ferocious tenacity paves the way to unlock the secrets of the dark nightmare: the demon unleashed.

Hanna's feet make imprints in the snow. Above her, dangling from a coniferous tree branch, is a tattered cloth as they make their way back to New Hampshire where they can stay to wait out the cold, harsh winter.

She takes the bit of fabric in her hands and turns it over to find the faint odor of smoke.

"It's either from a bonfire or..."

"Or they've been here," Diane pipes in... "who does it belong to?"

"This is a piece of Jace," Hanna says.

"How can you be sure?" Lucius inquires.

From the snowy bank they hear the groaning yelp of a dog – and to Hanna's amazement she sees Thor running up the embankment. He makes haste, howling to the wind, pulling and tugging at Hanna by her garments –

"He's leading you to something," Lucius says, and they follow suit, finding a boot buried in the snow and Hanna collapses to her knees.

"Jace!" She cries digging frantically in the snow. She uncovers his face; he is frozen and blue. She whimpers ... "Why?"

"He's been taken by damnation like the others," Bernard says.

Hanna tugs at his lifeless body, "But we are not far from the cabins... why couldn't he make it there?"

In the distance spanning an ever-darkening sky, the Ravens begin to appear and a figure, unlike the shadows, is pure darkness on the inside with seemingly flesh being on the outside – hands beneath a curtain of black garments.

"Jace?" Hanna says.

"This is our cue to go," Lucius says, nudging her to her feet, "we must go quickly…"

"But Jace…"

"He's a phantom of the night - Jace is no longer with us Hanna," and Lucius takes her into his arms carrying her away from the lifeless body.

Sixteen

On the Eve of the Winter Solstice a son is born. He has one half of a crescent upon his wrist; one half that has vanished becoming a single crescent with a staff running down the center. The haggard old witch with yellow stained, pointed teeth stammers through a wrought iron door, "The sign of birth is changing," the witch says, hunched and aged. Goldie, seated at a table with a feast the size of multiple families strong, and Leisha to her right, stands appalled.

"What is this? What do you mean?" She quivers, tossing her folded napkin onto the table.

"How can this be?" Leisha says, "when we have prepared for this baby to be born?"

"The child bares the mark of unity – only this child!"

"The mark of the other side … it has vanished."

"The great Lord of imminent darkness will be furious," Goldie says as the doors to Hell's gate forces open, screeching off the hinges. In the jutted landscape they live within the catacombs. The demonic entity stands before them with eyes of crimson, and a gaunt face, looking more human than before – when he was seen shape shifting into the beast – the beast that devoured Sterling – the beast that wishes to consume all that is love and compassion. He seeks a following but most intimately he seeks true power.

Back in New Hampshire their houses are being ravished by men and women of empty cavities; their souls, now turned to shadow, has been devoured by the demon who feeds on mortal souls – making him stronger not just by a following but by an internal nature to feed and consume.

Hanna tucks her newborn son into her chest and zips her Gore-Tex coat, "His name is Lucas Daniel," she says when she feels a warm sensation in her chest and abdomen – bursting forth in a prism of light is a handsome figure of divine light – emerging from the shadow is Jace who appears like the others – an empty body that is vastly dark on the inside. From Hanna's womb bursts forth the shining light and the birthmark of the crescent grows more pronounced and shaped into a cusp – like a precarious balance between good and evil.
"I am the Prince of Peace," the being of light says.

"I am of the dark," Jace chants in a monotone, "I am the representation of fear and sorrow." The Prince of Peace grows brighter, emanating a prism of glorious colors, "Then I am the representation of the healing of sorrow and pain."

Then, as quickly as he speaks he diminishes and all turns to dark. The houses of the Druid's Army are burning and the dark Army is vast in numbers – being both the empty cavities of bodies and the lost souls of mere shadows. They hold flaming torches – Hanna and Lucius lose what was made for them. The demon's servants turn their attack on the Pagans when in the distance there is a large stirring of men and women led by a large gleaming pentacle lined across the horizon.

"Appears to be the Quaker society of New England," Lucius says.

"Who?" Luther says

"What?" Bernard asks.

"They call themselves the Society of Friends. Probably from Maine. They converted as Pagans and Wiccans when they came to the new world – they saw a different order under God, believing we are all made of his inner light."

"In essence," Luther responds.

"And we are friends of yours," a voice says from behind as they turn to find a red-bearded man of masculine proportions.

"They took our mountain," he says, "the great mountain of this plane's ancestors. They have desecrated our sacred land."

Hanna watches as her home burns, "I thought they were afraid of the light," she says.

"In the underworld," Luther says, "but in the outer world it's a different set of rules."

On the ground plummets a Raven, thrashing, with the bird of prey upon its back.

"Sage," Hanna says, looking sullen as the Society takes up arms against the dark ruler's following – yielding attire of medieval armor – they slash through the torso of the empty one; the sword, blessed with rose water, cleanses the body of its dark presence and the body fades to a light glimmer like wax.

"They may be destructive but they are not invincible – they are merely renditions of their earthly bodies," the Quaker man says.

"Body doubles?" Hanna says, as Luther steps forward yielding his powerful sword, slashing through another body that gives way to the blade – like butter.

"There's no blood," Lucius says.

"But don't let them into your soul – they long to steal what they've lost."

"So they are separated by body and shadow," Hanna observes.

"Yes. The soul split from the body – a body that's merely gel compared to having a complete soul."

"Then the demon only cares for one thing…"
"And we are to find out what that is," Archibald says, raising his sword to a small battalion, moving onward to fight the despair of darkness and greed before them.

The Guardian of the West evokes the Goddess of the Storms, summoning her with a loud monotone chant; her face appears through the thickness of dense, dark gray clouds and she expels her tears over New Hampshire; the fires die but the homes are not salvageable.

"All is in chaos!" Bernard says, "All is in ruin!" He hollers over the sounds of metal clanging metal as the men fight in a battle of the Holy War the prophecy warned them about. Archibald and Luther lead the men into their land and cut through the thick of bodies that yield to the night; the Goddess pours her tears into a flood over the river bed. Vienna motions with hands that could move mountains ushering the water, using the forces of nature, to thrust water over the enemy – and they wash away into the river. They moan in terror as their wax like bodies turn to liquid – being flushed and drained from the torrent that is all around them.

In the same moment of victory the ship of the undead parts the clouds and hovers about them when the mass of Ravens flock above, swooping downward to peck and dive, and repeat their ravishing nature upon the Pagans and Wiccans who shield their faces with outstretched arms; the shadows of demonic proportions are expelled from the ship like leaping giants who also yield great swords.

"We are severely outnumbered," Bernard says.

"We are an Army with the greatest of light behind us," Archibald insists. "Keep our backs turned to one another," he continues, "leave no one open," and they form a great circle, a sacred omen of unity and begin to fight the beasts of men who have gone into darkness.

"It is our duty to make them see the light," Sydney says.

Vienna raises her fists, reaching toward the Goddess, and a rush of a tidal wave is thrust against the ship – alarming the demon within to a howling laughter – and he rises from the ship, spreading his bat-like wings and the ravens dive in unison.

Gladys uses the Goddess to create a torrent of wind – striking against the ravens, forcing them away from the Army. They splatter like melted chocolate into the wind and the demon becomes more grave.

"The Goddess has lost her home too," Vienna says, and the Goddess stirs again – but sending the ship to sail away in torrents of wind and rain.

With his arms spread wide the demon morphs into the terror of the gargoyle – half man, half bird, taking flight and scooping in to take her by the neck. Leisha and Goldie take their stance behind their ruler and snigger at her demise.

"I know why you have come!" Lucius shouts, leaving the circle. "You wish to spill the blood of true love."

"Oh?" Goldie chides and Leisha gives a wide grin, "what better love than that of a mother for her child," she chastises.

"Or that of a father for his son," Lucius pleads.

"Or a sister for her twin," Goldie sneers.

"That is the example of love and fellowship of the dark lord," Leisha says.

The demon morphs into a man, rubbing his pointed face, raising his brows.

"Another child?" He muses when Jace steps from behind slashing his heavy sword into Lucius's back sending him onto his knees – his soul departs and becomes devoured by shadow; his eyes turn to stark black like empty spheres.

"Oh God!" Hanna cries.

The atmosphere changes and the dark of night turns to a bright shade of sunlight and the lot of twenty men and women look around finding themselves back in the streets of Massachusetts.

"What has happened?" Hanna cries, with her son sleeping warmly against her chest.

"A time warp," Sydney says, and they all turn wildly – with a touch to his shoulder, Luther turns his back to find Chris anxious for an answer for the *Daily Prophet.*

"Tell us," Chris says, amid a gathering of witches, warlocks, Wiccans and Pagans – covens of all disciplines among them.

"Wait," Luther guffaws, "what time is this? What day?"

Chris drops his smile, "You just gave us a speech... don't you remember?"

"It's the Fall Equinox," Sydney says "we've gone back in time – with our memories intact."

"Will you be using the first Book of Prophecy of the second?" Chris asks.

"What second?" The Sister's Coven says unanimously.

"The Book of Prophecy Volume II," he says, with a concerned smile.

"Where is this book?" Luther asks anxiously.

Chris looks deeply puzzled, "But didn't you send it?" He says modestly.

"No," Luther says flatly.

"You must take us to it," Hanna pleads, "I am no closer to my daughter... and now my husband," she sobs.

"The army has lost their homes and many of them their lives," Archibald says.

"The same with my people," Herman says.

"They have burned our town community," Eva says.

"And ours," Diane adds.

"I'm afraid to take anyone to the main village," Herman says.

"We all understand each other's plights," Bernard says.

"Where is the book?" Hanna says.

"It came in the mail yesterday," Chris explains. "The reason I am here."

"Whoa," Sydney says.

"This time warp is freaky," Amber says.

"I'm sorry," Chris says, "I'm not following you…"

"There's no need," Luther says "we just need you to take us to the book."

"Yes, of course."

"Where is the Calvary?" Hanna questions.

"That we can't know right now," Luther admits.

"Is this divine intervention?" Amber inquires.

"All we know is the lot of us are present," Archibald explains, "and we are no longer in the company of the following."

"Whoa," Chris says, removing his ink pen, "you all have experienced something for sure," he says, "can I have an interview?"

"Have you read the book?" Luther asks, looking anxious.

"The first page is about all."

"And?" Archibald says, "Can you tell us anything?"

"Just what you have said… the following will perish under new ruler-ship and the dark with embark in an immense ship, leaving the underworld to reign over the outer worlds – no longer to dwell in the catacombs, and I really can't remember anymore… but you're telling me… what's in the book …. It's real? This stuff is really happening?"

He bounces on his toes slightly looking overly zealous.

"The Book of Prophecy has obviously been written by a great Prophet. Likely a sorcerer," Archibald insists.

"Do you believe it was Tully who sent that book?" Hanna wonders.

"Perhaps," Luther says.

"The Holy War has already happened…" Archibald begins, when interrupted.

"It has?" Chris says, yielding a small microphone from his pocket.

"This is not time for an interview," Luther explains. "We need you to take us to the book. We must know its contents."

Hanna has the slightest twinkle in her eyes as she sees Sage – knowing the time warp erased nothing, but she looks to the sky above for a second chance.

Seventeen

Hanna glares at the pages of an open book. The pages slightly glow with luminescence. She scrolls through page after page that is seemingly blank until Sterling's face is beaming back at her; a golden raven is perched upon her shoulder.

"Hello, Hanna," Sterling says, not stopping so she can say more, "it is your time now – to follow your intuition; time to follow those deeply rooted instincts that is beheld by the care of your soul."

From those pages Sterling's beaming face dissipates and Hanna hears the call from Sage – alarming her that it is time to move forward.

"They want to spill the blood of true love," she says, "like a mother's love for her child."

"But Lucius has already relinquished his soul," Luther says.

"And Aly's father before him."

"Herman, we must go to your village – we have no other resources left – no other following," Sydney says.

"Yes," Herman says, "the dry period will be upon us. Again. We must hunt and feed our bodies that need to stay strong."

Matthew, Ned and Bill hang their heads, "But we still have our town," Bill says.

"That's right," agrees Matthew. "We are not without homes."

"What we are saying is that our friends are not without homes," Ned explains.

"Thank you all," Herman says.

"Yes, that is gracious of you," Eva agrees.

Hanna takes her son in her arms, presses him to her chest and begins out the door to find the streets of Massachusetts in mayhem. Through the streets of peril, where men and women argue in angst and men fight their way to dominance, Hanna finds a storefront like a hidden gem that sells merchandise for the Lore.

"The dark is invading their souls – taking over their minds," Bernard says, maneuvering past bodies that have fallen drunk in the street.

"The next page of the book," Luther says, "does it describe the reign of dark energy?"

"It says we have to follow our instincts," Hanna reproaches, stepping inside the store, hearing the clang of a bell similar to Sterling's store.

A woman with youthful features steps out from behind a curtain, smiling with her lips slightly parted despite the melancholy outside her door.

"How do we stay sane in a time like this?" Bernard says.

Inside, Hanna senses familiarity like a case of déjà vu, "Do you have a pentacle back there?" She says.

"Yes, I do," the store worker says passively, and they follow in Hanna's lead; she looks in amazement.

"This looks exactly like Sterling's sanctuary; she had a shrine just like yours here," Hanna points.

"I am an oracle," she says, "I have been channeling positive energy from a very powerful Elder."

"Do you know by what name?" Luther asks.

"I haven't received a name but the energy I feel is from some powerful beings made of radiant light which made me convert this room for the practice of divination."

"Can you tell us anything you have seen?" Bernard begins to ask when Luther starts shouting, "Lucius," he calls to the seemingly barren wall until he walks forward.

"He's having a hallucination," Bernard shouts.

"No, he's being called by the prisoners of the dark army – they have taken my entire army," Archibald explains, "now they want more," he groans, grabbing a hold of Luther by the shoulder when a deep vortex of a black hole opens before them.

Bernard leaps to grab a hold of Archibald's boot when the vortex becomes wider, "Stay back," Sydney yells, and Vienna and Gladys shield Hanna as the store owner crouches to hold onto a table when the vortex becomes a vacuum and Luther followed by Archibald are swallowed by the endless hole; then, the vortex closes, leaving Bernard's hand stuck as the women grab onto him, pulling with sheer might and the vortex releases his hand.

"What are we going to do now?" Bernard hollers, "What are we to do if an entire army cannot defeat the darkness?"

"We are not left with much of a choice at this point," Ned says, turning to Bill and Matthew, "I am afraid that we have lost the Holy War – all is in vain."

"You are right," Bill says, "it is time that each man must defend his own families … we have lost this war otherwise. Continuing to fight is of no use."

"We must not give up!" Hanna pleads.

"We are all very sorry, Hanna," Bernard says, "but they are right – we have lost the entire army. We have lost the following. The dark is just too powerful."

"I am afraid that I must go," Bill says.

"And I as well," Ned agrees.

"I will also be leaving," Matthew hesitates. "To check on the well-being of my family."

"I am very sorry about," Bernard's words fall away.

"About everything. I am sure," Hanna says, "and I do not blame you. I fully understand."

"Thank you," Bernard says with a nod and the men file out the curtained entrance and enter into the night where mayhem still resides on the streets like a raging arena of acrobatics – only more haphazard and less skillful; some fall from roof tops, landing in trash bins – drinking to a plundering wayside.

"Herman," Hanna says, "your village and your people may be my only hope."

"Our only hope," Sydney says.

"That's right," Vienna agrees.

"I'm still in," Amber says.

"As am I," Gladys adds.

Herman pats Hanna on the shoulder and turns to Eva; they both nod in silence when the curtain is drawn back and a powerful man stands before them wearing heavy trousers with a tight fitting army green tee.

"Drake!" Eva says, "How did you find us here?"

"I followed the path of a great warrior," he says, and bows to Hanna, extending his hand, "I sense that you have received the letter."

"Yes," she says.

"Then you might also have the premonition to follow me to the Shamanic town of Connecticut."

In the next moment, Sage pecks at the glass of the window. The store owner removes the heavy red curtain and finds the hawk panting with its beak open wide and its wings fluttering.

"The totem bird wants us to leave," Sydney says.

"I'm not sure why I can't teleport at my will," Hanna says.

"You have to use your mind to deconstruct your body. To become a light body. To move freely in transport – you must use the field of energy at your will," Drake explains.

A raven caws above and lands upon Sage with a menacing fright.

"Open the window," Hanna hollers, and the store keeper makes haste, letting the bird in while waving her arms frantically to keep out the totem of the dark.

Sage lands gingerly upon Hanna's outstretched arm.

"We can no longer go by foot," Sydney says, raising her hand to summons the spirits, "can you – I don't know your name …"

"The name is Tara," the store keeper says.

"Tara, can you stand to the North in the great circle?"

"Yes, I can do that," Tara says.

"We are going to find the doors of the light to transport Hanna to the Shamanic village."

"There, the book's contents might be revealed to us," Drake says.

But the ravens are stalking – ravishing the land and the people there. Boston grows in madness and Hanna feels more anxious than ever – she wants her daughter in her arms and she wants her husband back. How could the father of her daughter kill him so mercilessly? She feels something is amiss but it is time that she learn how to be a productive witch.

"We can practice the way of enchantment to start," Gladys says, almost too cheerily for the circumstances.

"What good can that do?" Hanna says with remorse.

"Certainly for the most obvious reason," Gladys begins, "we need to enchant the ravens."

"They can be subdued by the enchantment," Vienna explains.

"Then how do you suppose we do that?" Hanna asks eagerly.

"The allure of Singing," Gladys says.

"Yes," Vienna says, "to chant."

"Through incantation," Sydney says.

The women take their place in the great circle; Hanna in the center, Tara to the North, Gladys to the East, Vienna to the West and Sydney to the South. The Sister's Coven reside in a circle to the outside of the

pentagram and they begin singing *peace –
peace – peace* like the hum of fine crystal;
inside, the pentagram, the center and the four
corners chant *om* of the legendary Buddha.
An aura of light sweeps through the room and
swirls in an illuminating glow above.
"Now," Gladys says, "focus on the ravens."
At first, a lone raven, falls, subdued by the
cadence and rhythm of chanting. Then,
suddenly, each one falls toward the ground
with its wings outspread like a solitary
feather floating, completely entranced.
And the women file out the door in a single
file line, humming, singing and chanting –
they walk among the litter of birds adhering
to the divine sound.

Tara follows behind the enchantment
procession and points her face to the clouds
that are parting to bring out the sun. Then,
each and every one rises, taking flight to the
parted skies. And one by one they each
vanish seemingly into an oblivion as if time
has lapsed, and all is eerily still.
But the demon is alive, awoken. He has his
mayhem on New Hampshire and Vermont.
As a man he stands tall and lean, with a gaunt,
long and pointed face, and sleek black hair,
with eyes like slits that are charcoal black. As
the beast, he's a demon of the night with bat-
like wings and feeds on sacrificed blood –

those bodies continue to turn to an empty cavity and a shadow for a soul.

The covens have only witnessed the beast as it fed on Sterling – preferring the most animated blood but the people of the East have succumbed to the demon's wrath and are left with their empty cavities that roam endlessly with no purpose while their shadows, a mere rendition of a soul, is to adhere to the demon's wishes and demands. And Connecticut is no exception. He claps his hands and all take a bow – at their demise, Jace and Lucius follow suit and are damned to feed on the remaining blood as the demon points his face with a half-sided grin, relishing in his new Calvary.

"We are a thousand strong," Goldie says, with her pet rat upon her shoulder; she pats its matted fur.

"You must mean thousands," the demon chides and Goldie has a deep laugh aside Leisha, who stands proud in black, like a thick curtain over a wiry frame, and shares in the laughter of victory among the masses – they lower their heads as the streets of Connecticut become thick and dense, with the wrath of demonic possession.

Now in the daylight, Hanna and the Pagans and the Shamans recognize themselves to be in an altered state.

"Is this another dimension?" Amber says.

"Appears to be another time and place," Sydney says.

"The Elders must want us to see this vision," Vienna reckons.

"Perhaps not us, but you, Hanna. What do you see?" Sydney inquires.

"Oh, my gosh," Hanna says, lowering her bottom jaw.

"What is it?" Amber asks anxiously.

"It's Mr. Beecham."

"Who?" They say in unison.

"My science teacher. I was his student in the ninth grade when his science experiment exploded."

"What else?" Sydney asks eagerly.

"He had burns all over his body."

"Are you saying," Sydney begins...

"The students there would taunt and tease him... I could tell that he knew, so I asked him if he wanted a friend... but he never responded. Then he left the school... but of course I could not recognize him..."

"Are you saying that you have recognized him recently?"

"The gaunt face... is the face of my old science teacher, but I had forgotten what he looked like."

"You are telling us that you personally knew the demon ... and perhaps he has learned dark sorcery – especially to restore his face," Sydney seems to understand.

"That must be a reason why you have been chosen," Vienna says.

"I'm having a premonition – or an insight…"

"Tell us," Vienna says.

"That the demon can only be defeated by the great warrior whose sword is anointed in sacred rose water."

"But that demon is destroying all that is sacred," Herman says.

"Not yet," Drake pipes in, "we have our lands yet, and waters that have been blessed by the most notable of Shamans."

"I cannot believe that I did not remember…"

"But now the Elders are showing you in a cosmic vision," Sydney explains. "You're compassion for Mr. Beecham is the love they are after."

"You're the one then," Gladys says.

And the Pagans and the Shamans turn back to the night where Hanna finds Sage weeping.

Candace Meredith

Eighteen

Archibald and Luther find themselves back in New Hampshire where the dark army ravishes the land looking to take up new recruits; the vortex dumped them on soiled ground. Archibald glares at the empty cavities of his Warlocks and finds Diane moving through the land; he takes her by the waist and ushers her away until they can contemplate a strategy to bring life back to the men. In Vermont, the Shamans are nowhere to be found as their second home location has been turned to ruin; the once beautiful log cabins that lined the Green Mountains are rubble – Herman and Eva know they have no use there and that the community has moved onward toward home. In Maine, the Quakers return to find the greatest mountain in shambles; they make haste to study the legends of the Holy Wars and find that the tears of the Goddess over what was Mount Katahdin have become a great flood in the catacombs – her reprise to the demon for sabotaging her fortress. New England is falling deeper into despair as darkness invades their minds, their homes, their bodies and ravishes the sacred circle.

The streets of Massachusetts grow in fury; the dark engulfs their soul and the need to destroy overcomes the people.

The massive ghost ship anchors at the port of Connecticut. Following the massive vessel is a mass of gray-coated clouds that covers the sun in permanent retribution but the people do not know what they have done wrong for evil to make its presence. Even the waters are tainted by a metallic like mercury and the life there dies over.

"There is a portal," Hanna says, darting her finger toward the East.

"Careful," Sydney protests, "it could be a dark calling."

"But I'm to follow my intuition," she says, "and we must go there."

"We follow your lead, sister," Sydney replies and the women along with Herman and Drake enter the portal; they are guided through a tunnel of light back to Tara's store. "I forgot to take the book," Hanna says. "That must be why we have come back," she yells as if distance and space is immense among them. Through the portal lands Sage and Thor with a thud at her side.

"You forgot your totems as well," Sydney says.

"Yes," Vienna says, "we need the book, we must study its contents to get further knowledge about the destruction provoked by darkness."

"Certainly there must be more to it than to follow your instincts," Gladys says.

"I believe the pages only appear to us throughout the journey," Hanna says.

"Then the journey is open to interpretation," adds Amber.

"Like it's not already written," Priscilla muses.

"Then how is it of any use to us?" Paisley questions.

"Stay calm sisters," Sydney states calmly. "The prophecy has been written for eternities – we must trust inner guidance – that's part of the journey – part of the prophecy."

"Well said," Gladys says, "and Hanna has strong intuition – her premonitions can persevere to find her daughter."

"And now my husband."

"Your daughter's father … who we always knew was a dark one," Amber sniggers.

"He has turned his back to evil," Paisley interjects.

"That's what we said would happen," Priscilla chimes in.

"What do your instincts tell you Hanna?" Sydney steps between them.

"He promised to find my daughter."

"Well, he found her. So now what?" Amber says candidly.

Sydney darts her eyes and objects, "We should not just use speculation, it has no energy behind it, no precedence."

"Agree again," Gladys says, "and as guardians we are overseers of the elements, and we are here to use our gifts to help you Hanna."

"Yes," Vienna says, "as before we are still here to help you as we can."

"Air and water are strong properties. They make use of the Goddess' energies," Sydney says.

"And I am sure they will be of use again," Hanna says, cradling Lucas in her arms. "With a baby, expedient travel is vital... I need to learn more of the craft."

"I might be able to help with that," Tara says, tossing her hand in the air.

"We must remember," Reese says, from the darkened corner, "not all intuition or foresight will be exactly correct... perhaps that is why the book is precarious. We should use caution even with divination."

"Will do, Reese," Hanna says as she turns to Tara whose store is filled with candles, crystals, incense, books and spells.

"I believe we should enchant the people of New England before their souls are susceptible to turning to shadows," Reese says.

Back in Connecticut the demon steps off the immense wooden vessel with his hands raised, "I have summonsed you to the perils of your death," he smiles, flanked by Leisha and Goldie.

"He's building his army," Reese says.

"So we need to enchant those who have turned to evil," Sydney says.

"That would make sense," Gladys agrees, "we need to first turn back those who found despair in the shadows."

A warrior of fine physique runs with great intent through the population of Connecticut, who happen to be celebrating the coming of the New Year. Time cannot stand still for long and a lapse in time is never permanent. The people of Connecticut celebrate according to a traditional calendar year but the Pagans adorn their homes with crystals and orbs and celebrate the phases of the moon and honor the Goddess of Rebirth. The warrior Shaman raises his weapon, carried above the shoulder, aiming for what would be the heart if he were a mortal – but for a demon the staff must cut through the neck to the spleen – until Jace uses a basic sling shot and a rock to knock the warrior off balance, causing him to spill his weapon.

"Jace," Reese says, aghast, "he's stopped the Shaman," she continues, tearing a sheet of paper, writing with the tip of a quill.

"Automatic writing," Sydney says, "she's using telepathy to see events as they are happening."

"You are my faithful servant," the demon grins, extending his forefinger – and you are forever my captive," he says, pointing toward Lucius who kneels over the Shaman.

"If you don't choose to follow me at your will …"

"Lucius is caring for the fallen Shaman," Reese explains, her eyes looking glazed, peering steadily at nothing in particular as she continues to write on paper what can be seen by the third eye.

"They call this place a Garden of Ideas." The demon squints his brow.

"I see," Goldie muses.

"We have come with splendid ideas," Leisha utters between pastel red lips.

"No wonder the Shamans breed here," Goldie says, kicking up dust to the Shaman who is barely conscious and they leave him there are the sky parts, with all remaining dense, and black; the town scurries toward their houses but the dark army reigns from the vessel and the ravens swoop in, stealing amulets from their necks – protective spells appearing too weak to ward off the impending darkness. As the demon extends his arms, his body splits, forming two leathery wings with the feet of a crow and a face of stone – the gargoyle-like presence sends all fleeing from their houses and into their vehicles – hoping they can drive fast and far enough to reach the Shamanic village. The demon takes into his grasp the Shaman and parts his teeth sinking his razor-like fangs into his bare neck, and relishes in the blood of the sacred one.

"He is of the most evil," Reese cringes.

"But gargoyles are an ancient legend that are used to ward off evil," Amber says.

"It's likely part of his joke," Sydney muses, "nothing has been proven to ward him off either."

"Not the enchantments, the potions, the totems, nothing," Priscilla says.

"At this time all we can do is counter the hex with an enchantment. A spell to bring radiant light to the shadows of the dark," Reese insists.

And Tara unlocks a boxed chest, removing a book on the forbidden, spells – spells that could go wrong – and there is no counter-curse to change the results whatever they may be.

"Those spells are theoretical," Sydney says.

"They are our best chance," Reese says.

"They are probably all that we have," Gladys agrees.

"They may be theoretical but they are based on sound principles in the laws of the universe," Drake says, seated at a chair against the wall.

Herman nods and Eva covers her heart with her hand, "How else can the dark beast be defeated?" She says.

"Only by starting with the shadows, the followers," Herman says, "the beast has never been defeated so of course the spells are based on theory."

"The Shamans have used spells for healing and divination to know something of the impending weather – to survive – to till the grass before the rains – but never the need to ward off something so evil," Drake says, peering at the women.

"But the Book of Prophecy has been correct – it had been written by a witch just as these spells so they must be plausible," Gladys pleads.

"Then all we can do is hope the spells do more than our former enchantments," Paisley says.

"Our protective spells certainly didn't work," Priscilla agrees.

"Nonsense," Herman says, "the child is still alive."

"And she bares the mark of protection," Sydney says.

"She beholds the Goddess," Reese exclaims. On her way to the cellar, Hanna rips the book of demonology from the shelf turning directly to the ritual of the infant; she thumbs through the pages at a steady glance to read of the anointed pure infant; the blood of the infant shall spill over the boiling cauldron and when the demon drinks from the cauldron he will have immortal life and sole power over the dark that casts its shadows to reign over the light – then all will be gray and bleak. Suddenly *The Handbook on Demonology* is knocked abruptly from her hands.

"You mustn't open your mind to malice – being susceptible to demonology can turn you to a shadow," Sydney grunts, and kicks the book across the floor.

"You must always keep your mind strong, positive and in accordance with light energy."

"That monster wants to drink the blood of my child," she winces.

"But we are stopping it," Sydney interjects, "and you have split the two energies of masculine and feminine. I am certain the demon must have the energy of both to succeed… but he will never get that far."

"How did she get past your protection spells?"

"Goldie was on to us from the beginning – we didn't know that we were late. At least, as far as we know, she isn't hexed – maybe we can get close to her."

"She is mine. And I want her back."

"Unfortunately, we are all kept at a great distance – she's in the possession of a possessed witch of the most evil kind. And of right now we do not know where she is kept."

"If we find the witch we find my daughter."

"But if we stop the demon – then good can be restored even in the ones who have been oppressed. The demon seeks spiritual dominion by invading the mind and oppressing the spirit."

"I won't open my mind to the torment," Hanna agrees, "Thank you," she says, and holds her son closely, wishing her daughter could be equally as close.

"It is our duty to expel the demon," Herman says standing behind the women with the book in his hand. "I am of a strong mind," he says, "this book may be useful later," and he leaves to the cellar where the other women and Drake have assembled.

"We are still in the midst of a Holy War," Drake says, removing a smoking pipe from his knapsack.

"We are all aspects of one energy," Reese begins, "when that energy is united it is both equally masculine and feminine..."

"But those energies have been broken," Hanna interjects.

"Yes," Reese continues, "and so we are gathered here for the Charge of the Goddess," she continues as Tara burns incense and lights the candles at the altar; a large rose quartz crystal adorns the table.

"The Charging of the Goddess" will strengthen your daughter and instill in each of us her divine energy... Great Goddess," Reese begins, and they hold hands; Herman and Drake smoke from the pipe sending the energy upward with the smoke as they chant. "Mother of all," Reese continues, "we call on you to reawaken your presence within," and as she speaks a swirl of radiant light encompasses the room, whirling above the table in a clockwise circular motion, "we ask for your divine inspiration – to keep us strong in these times of great peril... take away all sorrow and fear – and give to us your eternal blessing..."

And it is then that the women begin to rise – levitating from the energy of the room like a vast blimp – or a hot air balloon – pulling them upward toward the ceiling and Hanna's head is thrown backward as she inhales the energy of the Goddess; she feels elated with positive strength; then, each one does the same with their head held back, they are filled with the radiant energy of the Goddess that illuminates their skin and they float, basking in the light when the sounds of wind chimes echo about the room and upstairs the lights go out.

On the day of the Yule Sabbat at twilight the demon takes full charge of the night hours – with the fullest intention to make the dark hours shed over the light – and empowering one follower of the night after another. All is dark.

Nineteen

"We must re-empower our magical tools," Sydney says, removing her amulet from her neck, "including our totem guides." Then, she places her amulet at the altar. Hanna removes her athame and places it to the right of the incense in the eastern corner to represent the element Air. She also removes her pendant given to her by Reese and places it to the south to represent the element of fire. Reese removes a pentacle from around her neck and places it to the north at the altar to represent the earth. Lastly, a chalice is placed toward the west to represent water – and the women begin the ritual to cleanse, consecrate and empower the magical tools. Above them they hear the clanging of heals upon the floor – their ceiling – and Sydney shrugs it off, "Don't mind them – they have no awareness we're down here," she says and Hanna pries open the cellar door at the sound of nails scratching, allowing Thor into the underground chamber with Sage lightly placed in his mouth, he releases her to the floor and she flutters her wings – ultimately unscathed.

In a clockwise direction they begin their ritual around the altar; Sydney lights the candle, using the candle wick to burn the incense and begins, "Divine light, by the fire, purify this altar… it is with purest intent that we have gathered here to perform the work of the highest good."

All around the room smoke from a pipe of peace relinquishes smoke into the air as the Shamans sing, dance and chant around the sacred altar. Hanna takes her athame and asks for a blessing from the Goddess of Earth; she stirs the water from within the chalice three times in a clockwise direction and asks the Goddess to bless her athame tool – to always be used for divination and other magical uses; she takes the blessed water and touches her son's head asking divine light to show them the way to defeat darkness; she uses the water to purify her own soul by drinking from the chalice and passes the contents to each coven member; together they cleanse and consecrate the sacred altar; they ask of the Goddess to empower their magical tools and ask to be blessed with the spirit of powerful deities. They then blow out each candle and move the incense about the room to spread the light through the element air; "May we have the power of radiant divine light as we end this rite?" Sydney says, and Reese extinguishes the incense with the tip of her fingers. Now in darkness they fully experience the aroma and locate their inner energy points – the chakra centers to further open their inner being to receive blessings from the divine. They thank the Goddess of Earth, overseer of the physical plane, to end the ritual entirely. Reese spins the crystal pentacle over each tool and each body making nine complete circles over each one and over the four coordinates of the altar by only the light of the moon – intending to fully restore their energy. Now with the intention of casting a spell they sit in the dark to the sounds of the footsteps above.

"I will go up alone," Tara says, "I'm the store owner."
"We don't know if they pose a threat," Reese says.
"No, just some customers I'm sure," she explains, opening a large wooden door that is bordered by heavy logs, "Here is an escape route," she points, "used during the prohibition to sneak alcohol into the store. It was a night venue at one point."
They usher themselves through the door down a long passage of dirt arriving to the other side at a modern night venue - but also one for casual dining and they decide to sit by a lit fire at the largest table in the place; they

order fine meals especially after craft work which makes them feel hungry. They are filled with illumination but solid foods feed the hungry body.

"Where can we perform spell work?" Amber whispers, looking over her shoulder to note if anyone overheard.

"We may go back to the cellar," Sydney explains, "remember the second book is open and we are expected to trust intuition by this point."

"All I have is butterflies," Priscilla says.

"I second that," Paisley agrees.

"We all do dear," Gladys assures her, taking a bite of salad, "but even among war, all we can do is try to live a little normal."

"As best as we can," Vienna agrees.

"As Guardian of the east and the element air I am adept at matters of the mind…"

"And I am Guardian of the west and the element of water. I am therefore adept over matters of love and relationships."

"Those are two keen powers to possess," Sydney says.

"What powers have we lost?" Hanna asks.

"The Guardian of the north, earth, represents stability, ironically, but all things now are quite unstable."

"And the south?"

"Unfortunately, fire is the overseer of power."

"But that's not too bad," Hanna says, "Elusha went alone – to be with a man who she loves."

"Yes, that is good – she no longer sides with the dark," Vienna agrees.

"That is all very good indeed," Gladys nods.

"As Shamans," Drake describes, "we are quite adept too at your skills in divination and psychic ability."

"Yes," Herman says, "we hope to foresee the works of the demon before others fall susceptible to the wrath."

"We do call to the powers of the spirit to aid us," Eva adds.

"Akashi," Sydney says.

"Right," Vienna agrees.

"Spiritual energy," Amber smiles.

"Then we all agree and have come to terms with our journey," Gladys says.

"And our destinies," Herman bows.

"We should act quickly," Gladys says, "this is the night of the full moon…"

"We can call on the energy of the moon in spell casting," Sydney explains.

"Exactly what is the spell intended for?" Hanna asks.

"To bring peace to the shadows," Vienna says.

"To restore their minds to their bodies at best," Gladys further explains.

"There's a cathedral across the way," a lone woman says, "always has its doors open," she smiles.

"Thank you," Reese says awkwardly.

"You may be looking for a missing child," she says softly with beaming hazel eyes and ashy brown hair.

"Who are you?' Hanna asks, nearly standing from her chair.

"Try the cathedral, child," the woman says, "darling," she excuses herself, "for you must be the child's mother… no longer making you a child at all," she says with a faint sparkle in her eye and skin speckled with liver spots.

"Thank you, again," Reese says more casually. "Stay where you are Hanna."

"But she knows…"

"I know," Reese interrupts, "even the Elders can be disguised but the dark is near," she says, darting her finger toward the black bird perched at the window sill.

"We will burn a strong message in a flame of a candle anointed with gold," Gladys says, placing her napkin atop her plate indicating she has finished her meal. "Ascribe in the candle the name of the leader," she whispers. "Perhaps we should go to the cathedral anyway," Sydney says. "We've already set the energies in motion," she explains and

Reese twiddles with her pentacle, appearing nervous.

"I don't believe all is going to come out okay," she hangs her head.

"Why don't we split up then? Half of us will go to the cathedral and the rest will go to the cellar to check on Tara," Sydney explains.

"Yes, we can do that," Gladys says. "I will accompany you to the cathedral, Hanna."

"And so shall I," Vienna says.

"We are as well," Herman says of himself, Eva and Drake.

"I prefer to go to the cathedral," Sydney says.

"But can you go with Reese?" Hanna argues. "To check on Tara? We will come back for you."

"Only if your intuition is telling you this is right."

"It is Syd. It is."

"Then my coven will accompany Reese back to the store cellar," she gives a slight smile.

Noticing that the woman has simply disappeared Hanna pleads, "Certainly she is, or was, a deity ... it's no coincidence we just evoked those energies."

"You are our guide," Drake says, extending his hand, gesturing to the open door and the lot of them file outside, the Raven taking flight, and Reese along with the Sisters' Coven file into the tunnel and traverse their steps through the dirt – back to Tara and the *Witches' Brew.*

At the altar of the cathedral is a gold candle that Gladys removes vigorously and withdraws a pin from her hair she carves Mr. Beecham into the candle; they all gather around and she begins the chant, "Goddess of Earth bring us what we desire …" they begin to increase the energy by moving in a circle around the candle and Gladys removes a paper napkin from her purse where she stencils: *possessed bodies be free – linger in the dark no more.* And she kneels center of the circle as the Ravens begin to tap rigorously at the window and she drops the paper napkin into the flame – she rises with hands over her head, and the Ravens caw, and more reign in – becoming volumes of black birds swooping in – they tap at the wooden cathedral door.

"The power of air," Gladys stomps.

"The power of water," Vienna claps.

"The powers of the four corners hear us," Hanna says meekly.

"Louder," Gladys says.

"Shout it," Vienna exhales.

"The powers of earth, air, fire and water! Deities we call on thee!" She screams.

The power reaches its height as the Shamans sing, dance, clap, and voice their sentiments to the Spirits.

Eva's voice is like a sweet harmony and both men sweat in the fury.

"May the light bring the power of the Goddess and so instill peace and healing among the Shadows by the strength of the Full Moon!"

And as their movements reduce and the raised energy reaches a crescendo the paper turns to ash and rising from its ashes is the Golden Phoenix: the Goddess of Divine Light; as she expands her wings she gives birth to the baby in her womb and Hanna throws herself to the child – mourning her daughter to the fullest extent.

"Consider your wishes granted," the Golden Phoenix says and closes her wings upon the child until both vanish and Hanna is left grasping at fairy dust – the light particles of the Goddess.

"No!" Hanna cries.

"Yes!" Gladys pleads, "First you have chosen to save them all, to heal them – there is still time!"

And outside in the dark, the Ravens, the Crows, the Starlings fight haphazardly upon the roof, among the window sill and upon the door when a door to the back of the cathedral mysteriously opens and from their sight they can see a darkened tunnel.

In the end is a spiraling vortex in colors of the rainbow and they reach the store with Tara inside.

Twenty

The *Witches' Brew* is ablaze; the dark seeks to obliterate all that is sacred especially that which is essential to witchcraft. "Demonology is at work here," Gladys says, removing a lip pencil from her sack; she draws a physical circle around the little store and the women link hands one by one. The Shamans chant to deter the Ravens and Hanna thumbs at her amulet to release the Sisters' totem; soon, the wild cat, along with Thor, are by Hanna's side and howl at the dark birds that caw in the distance, flocking to the tree line. As they form a circle they contain the blazing fire and move in a clockwise direction with Vienna calling to the Goddess of Storms: "Aid me," she says with her hands outstretched, "with the gift of water take away this fire for the great circle is an act of love." From the ever-darkening clouds the face of the Goddess appears, "Guardian of the west, overseer of the element water, I have heard you," she says and from the parting clouds a large body of rolling water washes down from above.

"Goddess of Earth," Gladys says, "hear me … send this water from the west to the east!"

She exclaims when a torrent of wind spreads the water over the flames, and when the fire goes out all is dark again.

"This is why we were told to go to the cathedral!" Hanna exhales.

"Yes, but you were right in protecting Tara." The women pile inside the rubbish and debris to find Tara huddled beneath the reception desk – "the Coven, they must still be in the cellar," Hanna says and the Guardians rush to the cellar door but no one is to be found there.

"The Sisters. Reese. Where are they?" Hanna cries.

"We aren't sure at this moment," Vienna hesitates, "we should check back at the cathedral."

"That's right," Gladys says, hoping to add comfort.

"Our energy is strong," Vienna continues, "they should be in a safe place."

"We have Rajah," Hanna says, "they gave him to me... they gave him to Thor... I do not know why they are so dedicated to me..."

"You have been chosen by the Goddess," Vienna says.

"The dark may have come to know the two energies of masculine and feminine have been split," Gladys says.

"Perhaps they are being questioned," Hanna says, "but we knew someone had come to the store. We never should have let them come alone."

"But what we have done here is very important," Vienna says.

"Tara, did you see the Coven?"

"It has been nothing but dark… I could not see who they were… by the time I found the light switch, someone set my store on fire. All I could do was huddle beneath my desk to evade the smoke."

"It's the burning times," Eva says – "but if the spell works, those dark followers should be having a change of heart."

"And manifest in light," Vienna adds.

"Let's head toward the tunnel and check back at the cathedral," Hanna says.

"I will come with you," Tara pleads, moving her chunky bangs from her eyes.

"We don't know that the sisters ever made it to you," Hanna explains.

"Then we must also check back at the Tavern," Gladys says.

Outside they take their chances but in the streets of Massachusetts they find, amid the perpetual darkness, a calm, eerie sense of peace; even the Ravens are soothing to look at as they fold their heads beneath a wing and take to sleep over the calamity. Gladys pulls open the doors of the Tavern to find inside the continuation of stillness and quiet; the bar is full but no one is speaking. No one is stirring. Nothing has been interrupted and she wonders if they are in a time warp. Their ritual for peace is astoundingly literal and Vienna almost chuckles faintly but Hanna turns about not finding one of the sisters in sight. She walks briskly through the Tavern but it is as if someone has hit the mute button on a remote no one is holding. She checks very quickly in the women's room but finds all is empty. The peace and tranquility of silence carries over to the outdoors where again the streets are bare, naked like the deciduous trees and she realizes today is the New Year – and the darkness is ever pervasive as thick, dense clouds shroud the sky – she knows there is a permanence in the night. She knows that even tomorrow no light from the sun will shine through the heavy drapes of the looming sky. The stillness just may be a façade for peace and she runs in a full sprint in the direction of the cathedral – finding the lights are on and the door is unlocked. Once inside she finds not a single body and winces over the empty feeling in the pit of her stomach aside her son who is wrapped in a sling amid her waist and chest. She then feels the sorrow of widowhood hit her like a steam engine that illuminates her senses; the animosity has died but so has the festivities – in the times of the dark age upon them she asks the energy of the moon to bring forth her daughter and behind her the sounds of heavy boots appears from the stairwell in the corridors behind the heavy solid oak door. It occurs to her like a subtle revelation that magic is its thickest especially during the twilight on the eve of a Sabbat. Both her babies are blessed to be born on the Eve of a Wiccan festivity – so long as they are not promised to the night. Now, she realizes her energy is strong and as she begins to meditate on that thought the opening of a portal begins to manifest in front of her – even if she was not born a witch – both her children carry the energies of the Goddess and the Prince; with Lucas in her arms she feels immense love and compassion and so she steps through the portal at the moment the wooden doors are thrust open and in stomps Goldie – her hands on her hips aside Leisha.

"She was here," Goldie shouts, "I can still smell the stench of peachy little pie in the air!"
"Then I'll just do what I do best and smoke the little witch out," and Leisha ignites each altar candle with the snap of her fingers, "you don't have to be a Guardian of fire to make a little fire," she chides and telekinetically moves each candle flame onto the drapes that adorn the cathedral.

"Every sickening vessel shall burn," Goldie says, moving to the front door that is thrust open – Vienna stands below the Goddess of Storms; the rain begins to fall and the wind starts to howl – the wind is brisk and Goldie is blown backward by the force of it. Leisha, the Guardian of Earth, overshadows the storm, sending an earthquake through the cathedral with the force of her fist, and removes a wand from her dress – and she motions to the Goddess with one swift flick sending her behind the thick, dense clouds that shroud the sun; the Goddess is defeated in her own skill and power.

In the force of the earthquake the walls begin to crumble. The cathedral collapses all around them – they enter a portal and vanish amongst the rubble. Vienna levitates followed by Gladys as the Shamans exit the Tavern and at the sight their heads hang low. In the rubble, rain and debris, Eva tugs at a knapsack – Hanna must have taken off her back.

There is a crowd gathering around the cathedral breaking the first bit of silence is the storm all around them as the thunder roars. The concerned crowd lure Gladys and Vienna back to the Tavern to get out of the rain. The fire crackles from within the crowded venue and in the dimming of light upon the wall, Sterling's face appears subtly "Open it," she says and Eva turns to the Guardians offering them the knapsack. Gladys takes the pack and inside is the first complete *Book of Prophecy* she thumbs through the pages.

"There are changes made," she says and opens the book wide for the rest to see.

"Someone is changing the prophecy," Vienna says.

"There are annotations in the margins and lines through the text," Gladys says.

"Something unexpected must be happening," Vienna explains.

"But the dark is a false sense of peace it says written here," Gladys continues and digs in the pack for the second book, thumbing again through the pages.

"The dark shall cast their shadows until they are blessed and banish oppressed desires from their shadows by the rituals of the East (Lord of Death) occurs."

"We represent birth and death," Gladys says…

"But that's not a prophecy," Vienna says.

"Perhaps we need to facilitate a definitive Cone of Power," Gladys continues.

"But we already have sister and as of right now we have lost out center, Hanna, and our North and South - Sydney and Reese!"

"We are a broken field of energy."

"Do not forget about us," Eva steps in.

"As of now our enchantments and spells appear to be working," Vienna nods in response to the Shamans.

"Then if we need to further build our energy we will certainly look to you," Gladys says to Eva and then to Drake and Herman.

"We are a part of the energy we all generate so we look to you to defeat the possessed and the oppressed."

"The energy has worked on the oppressed – but now society is like drones," Vienna huffs.

"It will take time for them to find their energy again – they are in a state of limbo and have to find balance again," Gladys says, "Just part of a process," she assures her.

"Then all we need is some patience."

"The portals," Eva changes the focus, "may need to be balanced too – the energy may need to be re-aligned."

"The tunnel to nowhere?" Vienna questions.

"Or where?" Gladys sighs.

"Something as simply as changing your mind can change your field of energy."

"And so too the Book of Prophecy."

"All a witch has is a field of energy to tap into."

"And so does a Shaman," Eva says.

"A vortex is a field of energy…"

"So have they changed their mind?"

"To where?" Gladys asks.

"To Connecticut – to help the Shaman people," Drake says.

Crescent Lake is beautiful; the Shamans settled there when the people of Massachusetts suffered as Heretics. They live in communion with nature and have been practically unscathed since the witchcraft trials. But the demon has no prejudice against ending the esoteric practices of evoking spirit. The spirit people are shaken; the demon sits awaiting the new arrival of his guests as he finds comfort in the region he calls his new home – brandishing the Shaman people as unholy and evil – deluding himself despite their misery. His throne is the Southern Cove of the lake where he takes refuge of an immense rock formation.

Sydney steps through a whirlwind of energy in a portal followed by the Sisters.

"Well, witches don't have to ask other witches how they find one another," Gladys says matter-of-factly.

"We were astral traveling – it appears our spell only did good in Massachusetts. Maine and New Hampshire are still in peril – the Quakers fight the demon's army and in Maine the Druid's Army, what's left untainted, are fighting the shadows of New Hampshire."

"Then the Druid's Army must be fighting among themselves."

"Yes. Those who have been oppressed by their desires fight their own army – they need to expel the bad energy."

"In some cases a discarnate shadow fights its own body – a confusing and hectic engagement of good and evil – body doubles that split themselves, or the demon's work did, and now the energies need to be aligned and balanced."

"We cannot, or have not found Hanna," Gladys cries.

"Hanna is a disembodied soul," Sydney says with grief.

"What?"

"What happened?" Vienna exhales.

"Well we cannot find Reese," Sydney begins, "but Hanna's disembodied soul is where you find the Elders and her discarnate body is roaming here, among the undead."

"And for Lucas?" Vienna whispers.

"It's likely that he is with the witch…"

"She was found by Goldie?"

"She didn't get far in the portal – they grabbed at her pack, then, the baby, and Hanna," she chokes "she plunged the athame in her own heart – she was pleading but we were too far to reach her – we had only the vision. Now, her soulless body roams in grief and sorrow."

"Reese knew…" Vienna says.

"So did Sterling," Sydney says. "In a Holy War the only permanent death is done by the demon," Sydney continues, "by the demon!"

"We have time," Gladys says.

They turn at once in unison to find Hanna, not as a disembodied soul, not as an empty cavity, but as herself.

"Hanna," Sydney shouts, "How is this possible?"

"What happened?" Amber yells, seeing Hanna holding the blade by the handle.

"I'm only cut to the rib," she says.

"We saw your energy split from your body," Sydney explains.

"It was only the shock of the blade," Hanna confides. She looks more wise than before. "I was out of my body and I drifted up like a floating feather and the Elder said I had to go back. That it was not my time."

"But Goldie must think you've…"

"She has that old witch," Hanna moans, still covering the open wound with her hands – the physical repercussion of remorse and grief. Now, Lucas is gone from her reach.

Candace Meredith

Twenty-One

"Don't lose hope, Hanna," Gladys says, placing a piece of tape over the gauze bandage. "We thought your body was left to roam with the shadows."

"I might have," she utters feebly, "if I hadn't gotten the rib in my way."

From afar they spot a woman running – she waves her hand frantically – it is Reese being followed by a battalion of shadows on horses – she has something in her arms. She screams, running frantically until she leaps in a great heap over their furious horses – levitating in still motion as the shadows are unable to slow their horses enough – she does all that she can while cradling an infant in a sack; she tosses the infant at the moment she herself is pulled downward to the ground by strong hands and Vienna, Gladys and Sydney together take a flying leap but in a flash behind them, a pulling motion, ceases the young baby and in the next moment he is in her arms – Hanna has learned telekinesis – a trait like Goldie's and masters the movement of physical objects at will. Affront a nearby mountain, Hanna's eye catches a glimpse of Jace standing in the tree line as he turns away and the shadows follow after leaving Reese for dead upon the ground.

The women look astonished momentarily but they rush to Reese's aid – her body is freezing and her expression is stone cold.

"They have her soul but not her spirit," Gladys says and they lift Reese onto their arms, carrying her lifeless frame to the brush. They form a circle around her body and gather together holding hands and begin a simple Drawing Down, the Moon spell to use its energy to create a magical charge to restore her inner self.

"Energy by the light of the moon," Gladys begins, "bring to us a higher energy to make this woman anew – give her divine light – draw down the moon! Draw down the power! In this hour be with her. Give her energy inside as well as out!"

Reese's body convulses slightly as her head is thrown back and the energy literally fills her mouth and the light returns to her eyes and color clouds her cheeks – she gasps, coughs, and then moans.

"I thought I was gone for good," she winces and her eyes roll back.

"Thank you divine energy of the moon. Goddess of the Stars. Of the Earth."

"Magnificent deities," Gladys says.

"Now come to me," a voice from within Reese says faintly. She coughs again and groans – "He's trying to channel his energy through me," she says, and sits up.

She darts both hands to the ever dark sky and shouts "Healing will be sent!"

And they croak a hoarse kind of laugh from the cosmos – convinced their Lord shall see no end at his fate.

"Next we bring together the power of the God and the Goddess," Sydney says.

And the sound of the baby sends them into the woodlands where they can summons, plan, and eventually meet the demon who wishes to be so elusive.

"We are looking for a peaceful, balanced life," Reese says to the cosmos with an authoritative demeanor.

"There are many kinds of death," Sydney says, staring at the stars.

"Yes," Hanna mumbles lowly, "like my husband. Like Jace."

"We are together on a vision quest – seeking spiritual rebirth for those who have gotten lost," Sydney voices with optimism.

"The air is frigid," Hanna says, not intending to lose focus.

"We can go to Danica's and my brother's house – we all call him Sacred Sun, but his name is Elijah – they have room for us there," Eva explains.

"We have all used a great deal of our energy," Herman says, "there is a trail that will lead us to the house – it's less than a mile to the east." On the trail, Herman begins to speak, "The Shamans' approach to life and the way we regard the earth is misunderstood and lost by modern people."

"But not to the witch," Amber says smiling faintly.

"We are both greatly different from the majority of the Western society," Eva adds.

"This is the spirit road," Herman says, "and we are on a spiritual journey."

"And we practice Shamanic sorcery under the belief that in order to obtain harmony in life is to find the beauty in most things," Eva explains.

"Your practices are in harmony with a beautiful life," Sydney says.

"And it is so beautiful for you to help us," Hanna agrees.

"It is now that the outer world wants to take control of this life," Drake joins the conversation. "But on this trail we walk in beauty – and we shall seek harmony to neutralize those problems and then we all must live a beautiful life."

"This talk has made my heart glad," Herman says, and they reach the front door; before knocking, Danica, Eva's sister-in-law opens the door, extending her arms in an embrace.

Danica is a picturesque tribal woman with sleek black hair and raised eyebrows. She welcomes the coven and the Guardians, Reese and Hanna, looking them both in the eyes; "You have seen the spiritual plane," Danica says to Hanna, "and you have escaped imminent death," she says to Reese. "Surely the dark shadows will be coming for you," she says, guiding them to a large table in the gathering room.

"This is the space for initiation," she says, "you may want to know the way of the Shamans before you work with the Shamans," Danica continues, "you have learned sorcery, or the way of magic, you are therefore in charge of powers that could hurt others, but you have chosen the path of the goodness we all have in us – so we know that we can initiate you as a Shaman so that you too can protect our people."

"We are honored," Reese says.

"Yes," the others follow.

"The initiation begins with fasting and asking for help from above," Elijah takes over.

"Then, at midnight, they stand in the water of the frigid cold after ingesting an herb that causes hallucinations – if you can defeat those hallucinations – then you can defeat the enemy."

One by one they wade into the water; they open their mouths and ingest the herbs, not minding the flavor, and by the hour the hallucinations come; invasive serpents swim by a three legged goat that passes through the brush, then, the monsters and the demons come; they stand their ground for each one without having a sword to draw upon – then, finally twilight comes in a subtle form of grayness and they have long been too in-shock by the cold – but Danica rushes them inside, warms them by the fire and gives them hot cider to shake off the bitter cold. Then, they discuss what they could see and hear and how they had to stand their ground and let the night terrors pass them on by.

"You have been tested in the control of your fears and self-control in front of the demon – the demon that feeds on the inner soul of the person it claims – knowing self-control can keep you alive," Elijah explains, and sips from a hot cup of tea.

"This place has so much spiritual energy – how can a demon be present here?" Hanna asks.

"It's all in what he has come for – he must be seeking something or someone, something significant and special."

"We hope to have a clear channel to learn exactly what the demon wants – or why," Sydney explains, looking to the others.

"The way to clear the mind and to receive clear energy clairvoyantly is to head to that mountain top, after a day of fasting to receive a vision."

"I'm trying to find my daughter," Hanna says, "but this Holy War is a strong hold over my baby."

"You need to maintain the spirit of the warrior."

"I'm trying – but they almost got my son as well; had it not been for Reese and the sisters…"

"Then the warrior energy is shining through."

There is no light in the day and the January frost is freezing, but Hanna sets out alone after borrowing a thick fur coat that Danica had tailored from Elijah's hunt. She wraps her baby in wool blankets strapped in a leather satchel upon her chest and she heads to the mountain where her quest should lead to a compelling vision – hoping to see her daughter.

The only creature Hanna sees is a lone rabbit and it doesn't take long to get comfortable, as best as she can, with Thor laying beside her on a thick throw she brought in her knapsack – despite feeling weighed down she is determined. She smiles faintly at the site of Sage on an above branch and not a sight of the Ravens.

She fasts on the mountain top for three days about ready to give up when she opens her eyes, upon having no vision, and she sees a fox – making Thor run beyond the brush, and she laughs; she situated her baby son on her chest and closes her eyes softly. She finds the mellow ruffling of Sage's feathers to be comforting and then she has her first glimpse – a mountain top, a sacred circle, and the blazing fire atop the mountain. She wants to dig further so she takes a slow breath, and focuses on the exhale when the word: "Beltane" comes into her view and she meditates on just that thought – it's his birthday and a small voice says, a little girl, a girl who knows him well – it's his sister – Leisha. Then, another voice calls and the vision becomes momentarily unclear; Hanna tries to focus on the festivity of the Beltane being the beginning of summer – then she sees Mr. Beecham, burning in the flames at the science center of her high school. Beside his hospital bed is the little girl who her mother calls Leisha – a girl about fifteen years younger. "Leisha is his sister," Hanna says aloud, opening her eyes, and loses the vision.

"There is to be a festival atop the mountain on the date of April 30th during the Beltane Sabbat," she exhales at first finding no one in the room.

"They have gone off hunting," Eva says.

"It appears these are the times of dark sorcery," Danica says, helping Hanna remove her coat.

"We wondered when you would be returning," Reese says.

"What else do you know about the Beltane festivity?" Sydney asks, taking a seat aside her on the sofa, as she helps Hanna with the heavy pack; Hanna tells all that she had envisioned atop the mountain.

"The Beltane is the day of his birth – an honorary of the Sun God but he has gone astray."

Sydney shakes her head. "And his sister stands beside him," she says.

"But why Goldie?" Amber questions.

"A distant cousin?" Presley says.

"A family lineage?" Priscilla nods.

"It seems to be making partial sense…" Gladys adds, "your daughter is the birth of the chosen feminine energy … and you are the one who showed him love in his lifetime."

"He wants to spill the blood of the chosen one – the most significant love of all – on the date of his birth – a birth and a re-birth," Sydney says.

"But Lucius helped you to not only split the two energies - but to re-define love," Amber says emphatically in understanding of her revelation.

"So Goldie has made her sacrifice," Sydney continues, "she broke the bond of unconditional love between siblings, and not just that – twins."

"Breaking the bond of love feeds their negative energy," Priscilla says.

"Your son's birthmark is most intriguing," Danica says, putting her index finger to his clenched fist.

"The symbolism of the staff relates to the Elders and the half crescent signifies one of two energies," Sydney explains.

"What two energies?" Eva asks.

"Masculine and feminine," Sydney explains.

"To represent the God and the Goddess," Reese adds.

"They call themselves the Goddess of Celestial Light and the Prince of Peace," Hanna explains.

"Your sorcery and magic is meant to harmonize that balance – not just masculine and feminine – but good and evil," Danica says.

"So the mark is sacred," Eva says.

"Yes it is," Reese says.

"This is a delicate situation," Gladys says, and Danica and Eva nod in understanding.

"It is indeed," Sydney says, taking the sleeping baby giving Hanna rest.

Twenty-Two

"So he's just waiting," Sydney exclaims, "he's just waiting for the date to arrive – to devour the blood of the purest in nature – to make himself immortal and to have infinite power."

"Surely that power has been obstructed," Hanna says.

"Yes. Lucius was correct," Reese says.

"The incubi wants total, pure blood, but isn't something missing?" Gladys says.

"We're not certain," Sydney begins, "splitting the energies divides the power – the demon won't have the fullest energies."

Vienna nods in understanding.

"So he is to do this on the date of his birth?" Amber asks.

"Likely – because he's banished sunlight, twilight doesn't apply to him."

"But how? I don't understand how he has brought on the darkness," Amber moans.

"He is using the Goddess of Storms after desecrating her mountain."

"But we have evoked the same Goddess," Paisley says.

"Yes. So she could pour her tears – she is crying just the same."

"But a demon would never cast a great circle?" Priscilla says questioningly.

"The darkness mimics the sorcery of the light," Vienna says.

"Then the dark is planning a Satanic ritual?" Priscilla adds.

"Dark sorcery," Sydney says, "and Satanic under a different kind of cult."

"The upside down pentacle," Priscilla says.

"That's right," Sydney says. "The creator of dark magic desecrated the sacred pentacle, the pentacle used to evoke the light – by turning it upside down, and giving it a demonic presence – complete with horns."

"So they continue to desecrate," Gladys groans.

"That they do," Sydney says.

"And they plan to do the same with my baby," Hanna sobs, too choked up to speak more clearly.

"They seek to break the bond between true love," Amber says, looking to Lucas.

"Precisely why the men have left for the dark side – to break that bond," Priscilla questions.

"But what does that prove?" Hanna asks.

"We are not real certain quite yet," Gladys admits.

"Can we subdue a demon? Like we did with the oppressed and the Ravens?" Amber says, feeling slightly optimistic.

"Highly doubtful that a simple spell will expel a demon," Gladys says.

"A demon is just too strong for simple magic," Sydney agrees.

"It will take a great imagination, creativity and awareness," Danica chimes in, "in our practices we have learned of the sorcery produced by dark energy and countering that energy is complex and can be disorienting to challenge."

"But we created an entire army and a following to fight and defeat the dark others," Hanna explains, "but in truth, sometimes less is more."

"But we've already said a simple spell won't work," Amber trembles a bit, feeling flustered.

"But I also said that we must be creative," Danica says.

"We must figure out how to align the energies – to create balance," Priscilla exhales.

"But we are missing the sun," Amber says.

"No one said that this will be easy," Gladys sighs.

After a long week, the men return from hunting. An inexperienced youth, aged thirteen, busts through the door, exasperated – he exhales, placing his musket atop the table.

"Where are your manners, son?" Drake says, and the boy quickly removes it from the table.

"What did you see?" Danica asks.

"The beast was feeding on a large elk, or something, it had antlers."

"It has a field of energy," Drake interrupts.

"Couldn't penetrate it with our muskets. Nothing," Herman says.

"Did you try to shoot it?" Eva asks.

"We tried everything," Herman explains, "but we'd had to retreat – those shadows followed by the thousands and those birds were closing in on us so we had to leave the forest."

"We got only a single deer," Drake says, "very little meat in the forest thanks to that predator."

"The incubi can shape shift into that beast," Sydney says.

"And only feeds when he's shifted," Vienna adds.

"Come on outside boy, and learn how to find the heart and skin a deer," Drake says.

"Yes, father," he responds quickly and exits the door.

"The boy's name is Oliver," Drake says, then closes the door behind him.

"At least we'll have plenty of deer jerky," Danica says.

"But the thought of that beast being so close to us," Eva says.

"We have to figure out that field of energy," Sydney admits.

"To beat the demon we must learn from our environment – learning from what we have around us," Herman says.

"What can we learn from that elk?" Amber says.

"Not to get eaten," Herman slightly grins, "and that teaches us something the elk did not do…"

"What is that?" Amber asks, tilting her body forward as if she won't be able to hear well enough.

"To always be of a pack – never be one to travel alone."

"Ah," Amber says, with her face slightly illuminated.

"And to never run – but to outsmart the enemy," he continues. "We have to rely on what's within and use our senses to feel the energy vibration – then, we know when we are near danger."

"Learn to be a sensitive," Sydney agrees.

"Yes. Like being sensitive to a sound or movement," Vienna agrees.

"Dead on, sister," Gladys smiles.

"You can feel energy come to you – that's your intuition," Danica says, "life is emitting energy all the time."

"So the demon has created an immense field of energy all around him," Amber says, and both Paisley and Priscilla nod.

"And it's up to us to deconstruct that energy," Sydney says.

Herman stands in the kitchen, facing the northeast, hovering over a bucket of water and herbs and sings a chant in his native language, then he blows into his pipe above the water. "This is the water you will use against the demon," he says, and so he entrusts to Hanna, a vile of water that she is to safeguard in those cargo pockets.

"Thank you," is all she can say, and folds a cloth napkin around the vile and places it gingerly inside her pocket.

"The cure lies within," he says and departs from the room saying no more.

"You all don't have to protect me in that way any longer. Always tell me what you know."

"It was a matter of appropriate timing," Sydney says.

"After you had some training," Amber adds.

Hanna departs to the outdoors, not excusing herself, and leaves Lucas in the hands of trustworthy Wiccans and Shamans.

She looks to the gray sky and finds Sage there being attentive so she thrusts up her arm and she lands there quietly. "Dear Sage," Hanna begins, "I relinquish you of your duties – but I ask of you to leave a single feather," and she sends the hawk back to the sky.

A single feather drifts in the air like a floating leaf in the breeze. Back inside, with that feather, she taps the third eye of Lucas' head and sings him a lullaby; she then burns a candle scented with sage and waves the feather left and right to cleanse her child of attracting evil and blows out the candle, waving the feather over the smoke four times to ward off any impurities; she then takes the vile of blessed water and empties the contents into the handle of the athame and screws the lid shut.

She kisses the candle she ascribed with his name: Lucas Daniel, and buries the candle with the feather beneath a pine tree hoping the spell will keep him well in the months ahead – feeling uncertain about her son's future and more distant than ever from her daughter.

Emptiness and sadness fills the people of Connecticut and throughout New England; the Wiccans and the Shamans know that they will need to increase the energy of the land and its people. Thus they begin by making offerings to give the locals – to the Shamans and the followers of witchcraft – instilling in them some hope during the dark times.
On one visit, Hanna meets an attractive young couple by the names of Enya and

Edmond. Edmond has eyes like emeralds and Enya's shine like liquid topaz. Hanna is perplexed by the enigmatic couple and learn that they own the ski lodge – but Hanna is fearful of skiing and feels slightly intimidated by their tenacity. Hanna offered them a baked apple pie and some jars of jam. They smiled radiantly and asked that she come inside to get warm.

"Enya bakes, too," Edmond said and Hanna noted the batch of cupcakes that were displayed on the table.

Today she is to meet the couple at the local tavern and she digs in her knapsack for an alternative pair of slacks and a sweater. Hanna leaves Lucas with Sydney and heads out for the tavern; she understands that the Shaman community is built around the ski lodge and she is to meet the people who keep the town together as they live in the lodges surrounding the town. Skiers rent rooms at the lodge and she feels grateful that they have opened their lodges to them. She knocks softly upon the door and feels anxious to be in the company of the couple. Her athame and her amulet have been left at the lodge.

Tonight she wishes to feel a mild amount of normalcy, if only briefly, and in this way she can check that the rituals and spells are effective.

"I feel that you have come to restore harmony and unity among our people," Enya says, placing some bake goods and juice onto the table; although Hanna thought she left these conversations with the coven in order to refresh her mind, she feels this topic is going to be important.

"Yes, between the light and dark side of sorcery," Hanna speaks, taking a seat at the table and helping herself to juice and muffins.

"This may come as a surprise to you Hanna, but there is a sacred secret that I must share with you."

"You have my attention," Hanna says, looking perplexed.

"The secret is about love…"

"Oh yes, we have talked about this topic within the coven."

"But not in the same way," Enya continues, "what I want to say delicately is that you must find love for the demon and embrace that love unconditionally somewhat in the way you feel for your daughter."

Hanna feels like choking.

"There is sacred power in the act of love; only you can learn how to restore a good nature through love. That is the way to harmony."

"Love over war," Hanna says, "our first attempt at war crumbled a mountain … we were following the *Book of Prophecy* … a book that speaks about love…"

"But the pages have been torn from the seams."

"Then it seems that someone else is taking the matter into his own hands."

"Jace," Hanna whispers. "You know about Jace?"

"Perhaps. If he is the kind who keeps his promises."

"I understand about love: that you may not love what that person is doing but you can, in a higher sense, still love the person."

"You are very wise."

"But this is not easy."

"Oh, no. No one said that it would be easy."

"I've heard that before recently," Hanna sighs.

"He is doing what he is doing out of love too… because he loved himself, he felt that no one could love him back. So he wishes to commit an act against another that he feels was acted upon him."

"But it was an accident during a laboratory experiment. It wasn't anyone's fault."

"Perhaps he is angry then with the higher power. Perhaps he blames the source of light for his troubles and now he wants to be higher than that power."

"Perhaps so."

"You are without magical tools this evening?"

"I am."

"There is no problem in that. It is good that you came to talk. And to eat." She winks. "The thing that is our strongest connection in life … now I must find love in this."

"Keep saying it until you feel something different inside. Try to salvage the good in him, and think about him often – we need to start seeing change."

The following day the darkness prevails as ever. Hanna wakes to a ceremony being performed in the greatest circle she has ever seen; the Shamans are praying to again see the light. Hanna feels instinctively that the sun shall shine by mid-summer, but her instincts tell her that she needs to travel alone. She packs her thermal gear in her knapsack complete with the fur that was given to her by Drake's family. She stashes a few flares, the athame, and Reese's amulet along with the coven pendant into her cargo pockets and heads out the door. She does not wish to disturb anyone and feels they will understand why she had to move on; the last item she grabs on her way out is a bag full of peanuts and fills her canteen – hoping that Mother Earth will provide the rest on her journey.

Hanna enters the forest, disappearing in the thick of snow and darkness when she hears a voice from behind her – an all too familiar voice.

Twenty-Three

"Sydney," Hanna says and spins her body, illuminated by a lantern with her baby packed tightly to her chest for warmth. Thor licks at her hand.

"We know you are leaving on a vision quest – and intend to go alone – but our knowledge can help you," Sydney explains.

"And we can, you know, watch your back," Priscilla says.

"Sure can," Amber agrees.

"We also know that the Druid's Army did what they could," Sydney continues.

"As well as the Shamans," Priscilla adds.

"The Beltane is historically celebrated on the mountain in lieu of new life or rebirth," Paisley explains.

"The celebration of fertility through fire," Sydney continues.

"And a sacrifice," Hanna holds her ground.

"But in ancient practice the sacrificed was a man who was used to represent a God."

"But not in the way of practice by the demon," Hanna bellows.

"Use us sister," Paisley says. "To help you on this journey," and extends her hand and the rest follow to form a perfect circle around

Hanna, each representing the four elements: earth, air, fire and water with Hanna in the center to represent the Great Spirit and the child.

"I know that Thor is beside me in hope that we find Jace. So if he's at my side then certainly all of you are as well."

"Then follow us to tell you more, sister…"

"What more?"

"We believe the Beltane ceremony is not just to celebrate rebirth – that is, the demon achieving immortality as a man, but they also intend on a marital ceremony."

"Then Goldie has found her place," Hanna drops her jaws, "and with his sister by her side. It makes perfect sense."

"Then perhaps they plan to sacrifice the child – not to achieve death – but their very own personal heir," Amber wonders.

"Then they all can be the immortal family who reigns over the people through the darkness," Hanna says, angered.

Together they take the trail toward the east peak where they break in the hunting lodge on a vision quest where Hanna can learn more of herself: to commune with spirit, to speak through her and to reveal to her something that may be amiss. She crosses her legs, her butt planted to the floor, and inhales deeply. Outside she can hear the hooting of an owl that allows her to relax for deep transcendental meditation. She chants *peace, peace, peace,* and takes another breath. Her vision begins with childhood.

"It's Jace," she whispers.

"Tell us what you see," Sydney whispers back.

"It's his father – with a belt – across his back. Jace has permanent scars. He's taking the belt over his back – didn't do what he was told he says – he didn't look for work – and they have no money."

"What else?" Sydney listens attentively.

"He's so menacing and tyrannical – this is the foundation of Jace's fear – the reason he left us, me and Aly, because he didn't want to be anything like his father."

"Then this is the part the dark side seeks to own. Darkness feeds on fear especially repressed experiences – it causes the person to feel hatred, then they pass into the underworld, like a shadow of the night, leaving their empty cavity to perish or walk aimlessly."

"I found Jace's body, in the snow, why can't he be here – I mean, even as a blank canvas?"

"Those whose bodies perish were fed on by the demon. He is now a phantom of the dark."

"My husband?"

"He's a blank canvas – hollow on the inside – he was not consumed by the demon."

"Where is his spirit?"

"If he is a hollow empty cavity – mere exoskeleton of his former self then his spirit co-exists – his body of the dark and his spirit of the light."

"Why has Jace gone evil?"

"You already know. Like Goldie, they have a past, a past that is desirable by the demonic entity that thrives on acquiring human life, or death, and using their energy as its own."

"The demon thrives on being both man and gargoyle – it gives him his power, shape shifting is his specialty like your intuition Hanna," Priscilla says.

"The demon has his body but not his soul," Paisley adds.

"Yes, But Jace…"

"You have seen why his fate is to the dark side of energy," Sydney says, "but our focus is on finding Aly."

"What else?" She says.

"The Prophecy is changing – that means that no witch could see what's coming…"

"We have lost the Warlocks, the following, the army, the Shamans and the Quakers," Amber sighs.

"Because they still fight the darkness. The darkness that is still consuming New England," Paisley says.

"Which is why I was to go alone – so no others would get hurt."

"But we are not afraid, Hanna," Amber insists.

"We are here to walk with you," Priscilla says.

"Join our Coven," Sydney says, "become our sister – represent the light at the center of our circle."

"You want me in your Coven?"

"Of course we do," Paisley says.

"Yes, of course," Priscilla reiterates.

"You are my only family," she says.

"What does your vision tell you?" Sydney pries.

Hanna opens her eyes momentarily and closes them again. She takes a deep breath and focuses on the steady rhythm of her heart. Then, she hears Sterling's words, "Their heart is in the right place," then her voice fades and she hears the sounds of her husband, "Not all things are as they seem. Always follow your intuition. Create a new normal - you are the receiver and transmitter of the light."

"Somewhere there is the symbol of the sacred feminine and I must find it," she says, opening her eyes fully, feeling internally that she knows what her soul must do.

A faint *I love you* is heard like a dissonant melody before she turns to Sydney, "So be it," she says, "I love you."

"I believe there is an energy source that has healing properties," she continues, "we just need to tap into it."

"Wouldn't that be a light source?" Amber asks.

"Perhaps. But what is light?"

"A cosmic aura – particles explained by quantum physics." Paisley ponders.

"That light source also has my baby."

"Aly is protected by the Goddess of Celestial Light – she embodies divine light."

"Then first I must find the sacred symbol of the feminine source of energy."

"You do have the masculine … the athame given to you by Lucius, perhaps he was on to something."

"It is apparent that the two energies – the molecular physical body can be split from the atomic body – the thriving soul."

"Then do you want to try bi-location, a body double – and travel the cosmos…but I'm not an adept," Sydney explains.

"Perhaps it's best to do what your strengths allow you to do," Priscilla says.

"There was something I stumbled upon many years ago but I had forgotten – and never went back to see it again. Maybe it is still there…"

"What is it?" Amber looks intrigued.

"I didn't know it then but it was a chalice but it was so sooty and covered in dirt, well dust, but I recall being drawn to it."

"Where was this artifact?" Sydney muses.

"My Grandmother, Grandma Ester, then she always told me to touch a thing – I played outside mostly – but it could be worth searching..."

"We shall try to find her then?"

"Oh yes, but she is my mother's mother, two of a kind, stern and strict – but I have a strong feeling to go there."

"Where is she?"

"She lives in a quaint studio apartment in Virginia. Perhaps that closet still houses all those crystals too."

"Was she a witch?" Amber smiles.

"She and my mother don't speak based on a disagreement – they have different cultural views – my mother is a dedicated Catholic."

"What else do you know about your grandmother?"

"Not much. She grew up very poor and she saves everything she has."

"Hello, Hanna," her grandmother says at the front door after several hours on the train; not being an adept, Hanna lacks teleporting skills.

"I knew it would be soon that you would find me," she says, "come inside, and who are your friends?"

"They call themselves the Sister's Coven."

"Coven? A Coven typically has thirteen members…"

"We are four," Sydney says, "enough to cover the four coordinates and now we have our fifth…"

"Is that you Hanna?" Her grandmother says, being eighty, she still glides smoothly across the floor like the slickness of a cat.

"Yes, Grandmother Ester… they have asked me to join their coven."

"It's been years, Hanna. Your mother took you away - you must have been only four – and you still remember me?"

"Yes, I do. At times I've heard mother Pearl talk about you to father, but then he left us, too."

"Your mother became more sterile than I ever was."

"I remember a few things about being here…"

"But you were so young then. Just a child… well, listen, you all don't have to stand there – have a seat at the table. I've been waiting for your arrival."

"Are you a witch, Grandmother?" Hanna says as they take a seat at the large round wooden table.

"I am an adept," she says removing a tea pitcher from the refrigerator, "I gave up a lot to raise your mother and three uncles, but when they were grown I got out my old Book of Shadows and had been practicing some rituals when your mother came in," she sighs, "and that is when she took you away. Didn't even allow me to explain – I guess she thought I practice dark sorcery."

"Mother raised me as a Catholic ... I know very little of the Craft."

"Folklore," Grandmother says, "some people just call it a fable."

Hanna smiles thinking of Sterling.

"But magic is as real as the moon and the stars."

"Can you teach me what you know, Grandmother?"

"I will and I can to a certain extent. But I have a friend of the Navajo tribe, Lakota-Rah, and I have asked him to show you the way of the spirit people."

"I have learned some of the arts from the Druid's Army and the Shamans."

"No army can defeat the demon of darkness," Grandmother Ester notices movement beneath Hanna's Gore Tex coat and lifts her forefinger – "what do you have there?" She says, "My third eye did not see this; I could only foretell that a lost child would be returning to me."

"This is my son, Lucas Daniel," Hanna says, unzipping her coat and taking her son into her arms – his wide eyes peer at the ceiling light. "I have another child. A daughter. Which is why I am here."

"Tell me what has happened."

"A very powerful demon has stolen her… his followers took her … we were to have a battle on the summit of Mount Katahdin but the darkness crumbled the mountain and sent the Pagans and the Shamans to the catacombs – most of the followers fell into a trance by the demon and became shadows of the night."

"That is grave indeed my dear child… how your heart must ache as mine had when your mother took you away."

"Yes. It most certainly does ache."

"I absolutely want to help you… but I am too old, but I can watch over Lucas while Dakota-Rah teaches you the mastery of the dance of the spirits and how to overcome the dark."

"That is most generous, Grandmother. And you have the sisters here to help you with your needs."

"We are certainly here for you," Sydney says. Grandmother pours five cups of green tea and passes them around the table. Each thanks her and takes a small sip and smiles warmly.

"Grandmother," Hanna says casually, "I was wondering about a few things you had in your closet."

"Oh yes," she chimes in, "you always did brood over those artifacts I remember," she chuckles, "well, you are a witch now. Go have a look."

Hanna places her son in the arms of his great grandmother, noting their resemblance and walks anxiously to the dining room closet – as if she had just been there yesterday – and turns the glass knob, hearing the creaking of the hinges and finds the space fully stocked. The sisters stand behind her gazing at the crystals, amulets, incense, two slender swords with bronze handles, an athame blade, pentacles dangling on silver necklaces, a ceremonial bell, an ornate wand, a cauldron in the center of the floor and Hanna's eyes gaze over the chalice among the goblets made of heavy metal, but the chalice stands out among them – made of rose quartz. She removes the beautiful goblet with trembling fingers and tears in her eyes – she has lost so much time with this woman – yet she has the power crystals and the chalice she has seen in her mind's eye. Hanna takes the chalice to the kitchen and her grandmother stops abruptly – she too with tears in her eyes.

"That is the chalice of love. Of unity. Of a sacred marriage."

"Who was it used for?"

"For myself and your grandfather when we both entered ourselves into the world of magic and became a unison through marriage. You will know what to do with it and how to use it when the day comes."

"My soul weeps since I did not keep the birth water…"

"It is going to be alright. In time, I suppose, all the energies will be aligned and you will know what to do."

Through the window pane of the front door Hanna sees the proud features of a young warrior smiling and holding a thick book with leather binding.

"That is my dear friend Lakota-Rah," Grandmother Ester says, and she unlocks the door, as a frost bitten air enters the heated indoors.

"Grandmother Ester," he says, and removes his coat, placing the leather bound book upon the table.

"Grandmother?" Hanna asks.

"A very distant relative actually," she says. "You grandfather was a third generation Navajo; his mother was of the Lakota tribe."

"When did he pass?"

"You would have been around the age of ten… he died from heart failure. A genetic condition. He suffered a slight stroke, then his heart could not bare no more."

"You have been alone all these years?"

"I have the tribe who reside close by in the hills of West Virginia; they left the reservations due to broken treaties in Alabama. They moved their families to be closer in spirit. Lakota here can explain more than I can."

"My ancestors left the South during the era commonly called the trail of tears and left the reservation to live peacefully among the wild. We hunt our own meat and grow our own fruits and vegetables. It's what you might call a happy, uncomplicated life," he says, with apparent dimples and sleek straight black hair and bronze skin. His eyes are like graphite – as if the smoky gray bestows the power of wisdom in his youthful age.

"How old are you?" Hanna blurts out before re-considering and Grandmother Ester laughs.

"Old enough to pick up some ale at the local market," she grins.

"That's right," he agrees, "and old enough to learn the skills of the masters of the temples."

"Like Egypt or something?" Amber says.

"The spirits of my ancestors," he says, "I've brought to you the legends of my ancestors who have braved during darkness, as I feel you are battling yourself."

"Yes," Sydney says, before Hanna has a chance to speak; "Hanna has faced darkness alongside the warlocks and the Shamans."

"But the dark continues to wage war never-the-less," he sighs and picks up his book in both hands; "this is what you might call a Book of Shadows … but it is just a well kept secret with no name in the Navajo and Lakota tribes."

"I am hopeful," is all Hanna can manage to say.

"The darkness does not care if you have come in peace – the darkness sees no boundaries – and it will take true art to defeat the terror that I feel in your heart."

"A demonic entity has stolen my child," she says.

"A demon is of the highest evil and has to be approached with caution."

"The army, the Shamans and the Goddess of Storms have been defeated," Sydney says.

"What have you been taught so far?"

"The Druid's Army has taught me military skills and the discipline of Thai Chi. The Shamans have taught me practices in ceremonial rituals and the covens have taught me the way of the Craft – how energy can be used and manipulated by using ointments, rituals and spells."

"All of that is good practice and good learning. They are all necessary preliminary steps in learning how to defeat a dark enemy."

In the next moment, Lucas cries and Hanna is startled. She moves across the room and takes him into her arms, cradling him upon her chest, and he quiets – being soothed by the softness of her skin.

Candace Meredith

Twenty-Four

Much of New England has succumbed to the dark. Darkness reigns over the inhabitants who fought but lost their way to the shadows. The enchantment spells have worn and no longer protect the pagans of Massachusetts. Tara no longer has a store and calls upon the coven telepathically during meditation which has been received by the coven. In the spare space of the studio apartment, upon the loft, the sisters open a portal with energy summonsed by the circle during a ritual. Tara enters the vortex with her fingers bleeding – as she had to climb her way from within the Tavern as too many fights were an endangerment to her security. Reese and the Guardians passed a message through her that they have gone on to stay in Connecticut where they will wait for Hanna and seek refuge with the Shaman community. In the witch's catacombs, flooded by the Goddess of Storms, the baby cries alone in a cradle of sticks and burlap. The witch spats onto the board she uses with runes and sees death overshadowing the outer realm and relishes in its supreme power – anxiously awaiting the turn over for power. In the cavernous dwelling of the jutted mountains in Connecticut, the demon feeds on the blood of the fallen Shaman warrior from a goblet made of igneous rock as he marvels over the flames of New Hampshire – not yet touching the town of Connecticut as he paces between the two women who calm him with optimism.

"The terror will be delightful," Leisha says, soothing him in a dark monotone and Goldie cannot wait to grasp the sheltered child – giving her to his dark presence – through her sacred blood he will become immortal, in a human body, as well as the gargoyle – ruler of the night. He does not sense the presence of the Guardians but feels Hanna's strengthening power and he ambles not with fret but with pleasure as her blood too will grace him with ecstasy like he's never experienced before.

Hanna sits motionless in a tipi erected on the mountain of West Virginia. Lakota-Rah smokes from a sacred pipe and hands it to Hanna.
"You don't inhale," he says, "you let the smoke roll off your tongue and it reaches the heavens and the spirits – masters of the temples.
"It has many names," Hanna says.

"But we all argue on the fact that there's beings of light in the cosmos who hears and responds to our prayers."

"I agree as well," she smiles as the smoke rises above and she looks up to an opening at the top wondering if there will be light again.

"If you want my help you are going to have to trust me," he says, removing a jar from a pouch, and inside that jar is a small snake.

"If that demon wants your blood then he is going to have to pay a price…"

"I'm very afraid to ask."

"In this jar is our brother the snake, its venom has killed mature horses."

"Then what are you going to do with it?"

"Again, you have to trust me. I'm going to burden your blood with this venom – the toxin will be lethal but for you I have the anti-venom."

"Honestly, this is kind of scary," she whispers.

He takes her by the forefinger, prying her loose index finger from the rest and fits it gingerly into a hole on the top; upon entrance, she squeezes her eyes shut and feels the bite of two deadly fangs on her finger and he then removes her hand from the jar.

"We have tainted your blood – now the demon is destined for a deadly disease," he says, helping her to lay back as her body begins to perspire. She shivers.

"Now the venom is circulating in your body, feeling it move through your veins…" and he then removes a syringe from his pocket and removes her Gore Tex coat and injects the anti-venom into her bare shoulder.

"It will work any moment now," he says smoothly and smokes from the pipe. In the next moment she stops moving – small convulsions turn to slight tremors and then they cease. She blinks her eyes to know that she is still alive.

"Now," he says, "you can read from my book of shadows to know how my people fight evil."

After an hour, she can stomach reading. She reads about skinwalkers – the Navajo demon: a witch who has become a master but uses his or her powers for evil and can transform into an animal to inflict pain onto others; the skinwalker elicits much suffering and gains great recognition by committing the most evil of crimes – such as killing a close family member.

Hanna cannot believe the similarities of the legend and continues reading; the legend states that upon learning of a skinwalker it is the duty of the seeker to identify the skinwalker by his or her full name – then, the skinwalker will perish. "Mr. Beecham," she whispers to herself, not knowing his full name, "but he changes shape and preys, specifically on the blood of others…if only to end this just by identifying a name…"

"We Navajo," Lakota-Rah speaks, "do not talk of the skinwalker, so I had you read of the legend, then you can decide how to overcome its evil deeds."

"But I bet most don't believe…"

"It is for you to believe – it is your destiny," he says and exits the tipi into the dark night.

Upon reaching the studio, only lights flickering illuminate her way to the door marked: J. And she thinks of Jace, and settles down, into the couch, taking her son from her grandmother's arms and she lays down firmly with her son upon her chest and begins stargazing in reverie of the day she was born as she has learned from the book of shadows. Hanna, alone in the hospital – wishing she has met the sisters. But she had not. And she was alone with the best gift at her side; she wonders what she did wrong to deserve losing her – then, the dark shadow enters her dream and the air all around them becomes cold.

Not again, she thinks, and winces in her sleep. The Shadow brings a deep fog about the house when a faint light shimmers, hovering over the shadow – a mere silhouette of a man – and the spark of light grows brighter – An Elder appears who stands about the room with grandiose and a calm demeanor and the fire in the chimney grows hotter; the dark shadow retreats into the cold of the night out the window and the Elder speaks not forcefully but with great conviction, "I am Grandall, master of the Sacred Temple," then, the tall figure of the man in the shining wardrobe, and a satchel about the waist, lined in gold, vanishes and the dark scares her no more.

She wakes immediately sensing that the room is dismal compared to his grandeur, and she misses his vibrancy and warmth. In the hours that come she tells the sisters and Grandmother Ester all that has transpired, seated at the round table.

The grandmother nods. "And so now you know what to do," Ester says and Hanna takes a deep breath, and on a slow exhale she feels slightly calm, as if before the nightmare can get any worse. She laments quietly on a name knowing it just cannot be so easy but it's a step she will have to take to unfold pieces of a puzzle like the labyrinth of discovery.

Outside the temperature has dropped to freezing and she has not heard word from the

Guardians that the Shamanic town of Connecticut has been seized by the demon. She then ruminates that the demon is not just in hiding (if hiding at all) but is in a kind of hibernation; she speculates that an entity of the underworld would feel in its place with frigid weather but the catacombs do not see frost – the air is cool as to preserve mummified bodies but freezing is another story, and she wonders if now should be the time to seek out the demon if she gathers a hunting party. In her mind she doesn't exactly know the next step and takes up the topic with the sisters – with Tara added to the coven.

"Why is Grandall unable to seize the demon?" She blurts out at the table and Amber shrugs slightly seated in front of the hot pot pie.

Sydney finishes chewing and swallows her pie down with a sip of green tea before answering, "Grandall is like the master of the temple Lakota spoke about … he is a master of the light, not of the dark. Just think that perhaps without proper steps taken the dark could overpower the light."

"I can't imagine anyone defeating such a magnificent being."

"But you also could not imagine a sister watching as her own sister dies – that's the kind of power, or evil, we are speaking of and Grandall's not a fool who will lose Celestial Light for being unprepared and failing because it was not the right time."

Hanna digests more than her food and gulps – she is the one to learn of the right next move. She is too choked up for words. More now than ever she wants her husband. She wants the wits of Jace too, and soon she drifts back to sleep with those thoughts. While star gazing Hanna feels a different kind of sensation and senses a popping vibration at the solar plexus. Star gazing leads her to the public library where she can search the archives for news articles and begins with the year she was in ninth grade; a decade has gone by like a brisk breeze. She turns the pages of the news articles that have been made digital to keep up with emerging media and there she finds his familiar face with scarring burns beneath the name: Herschel Lambert Beecham. *But how has he transformed?* She ponders, and reads the article detailing the extreme surgical procedure he is to undergo to repair his scarred features – but even then, as the man of the demonic façade he is much different in appearance.

Perhaps, she thinks, *the façade is a transfiguration of his own deeply rooted desires that has blossomed from his evil calling. He has become the thing that he wants and dreams about most.*

Grandmother Ester draws closed the blinds and the curtains. She covers Hanna's sleeping body with a quilt and feeds Lucas with a bottle. She hums a lullaby and meditates with him in her arms – praying for peace. She senses the tranquility of the moment being around her granddaughter and hums the rhythmic sound until Lucas too falls asleep quietly in her embrace.

The following day, Sydney takes notice that something is different about Hanna but doesn't concern herself too intimately with Hanna's affairs feeling that Hanna's place as the Chosen One is rooted in her lineage as a witch whose genetics stems from an adept maternal grandmother.

"He has found his inner strength through the persona of a demon," Sydney says, "and the gaunt face in which you describe is a façade to conceal the scars – however the transfiguration takes place."
"I know his full name," Hanna says clearly "and I do not want to summons that name until I know that my daughter is safe."

"She must then be in the possession of the demon – it must take place at once."

"Yes, he must see himself for who he truly is…"

"Leave the façade, the mask, and identify with the true self through love and compassion – to bring forth the inner beauty."

"It is the only way."

Outside is night. It is always night. But not even the demon can block out the stars. The stars are abundant and the illumination by the moon is omnipresent setting the mood always in favor of the Goddess who gave birth to creation. Sydney and Hanna glare at the stars in awe at the beauty despite the frost.

"The demon cannot hide the stars," Sydney says.

"Star gazing in the cosmos is ever present," Hanna insists.

"You have been star gazing?" Sydney says when Grandmother Ester exits the front door.

"He is crying. I cannot console him," she says, and rushes inside.

Hanna goes to her son, places her hand to his head and caresses his fine hair.

"He looks like his mom," Grandmother says, smiling.

"But he does have his father's features. I can see in him," she says, feeling somewhat empty inside with a burning sensation in her abdomen just behind her naval.

She senses her daughter reaching for her – wondering if Jace or Lucius have seen her – have touched her or embraced her; her daughter is losing the sense of touch from her mother and Hanna wonders if, through Lucas, there is a sibling connection – if she can feel her fingers caressing the fine strands of hair.

Hanna takes Lucas Daniel into her arms and peers into his face searching for the light within when she sees a glint of light in the black pupils and she feels certain the entity within is aware of her success in star gazing. His birthmark, like his sister's, has no pigment as the faint white flesh bares the half crescent and a staff running down the center; *he must have half of what she had,* Hanna thinks, *then Lucius was right – and the two polar energies are now represented through siblings* and Hanna searches to know precisely how to find her daughter – or which to find first: Aly or the demon?

And why hasn't the demon found her?

Twenty-Five

The coven exits a vortex at the Shamanic town nestled in the mountains of Connecticut.

"Star gazing has enabled you to teleport smoothly," Sydney says with the coven including Tara dressed in preparation of a blizzard.

"The town thrives on these conditions as they manage the ski resort – it's the essence of the people. Thankfully the demon has not touched this place," Hanna says pointedly as if perplexed and semi-annoyed.

"I think she ignored you," Priscilla laughs slightly.

"We need to find the Guardians," Hanna continues.

"I think she just ignored you, too," Paisley pipes in.

"It's all business from here then," Tara says, as if finding her voice, "the demon must not seize another town and set fire to these people's homes – their way of living."

"They have already desecrated the lodges of New Hampshire," Hanna adds, "and you are right."

"That demon took my store – my only source of income – what am I to do now?"

"He took Sterling's life," Amber says.

"He has taken from all of us," Sydney interjects, "we are all witches of Celestial Magic and we all stick together – it is time that we figure out precisely how to stop a demon – one whose soul was internally damaged and his physical body scarred."

"He murdered because he has suffered," Amber says.

"And now others suffer," Priscilla agrees.

"Then we must find out how to heal," Tara admits, looking stern and solemn at the same time.

"We are each other's family now," Hanna says, with Lucas strapped to her body to keep warm, "and that's what the demon longs to destroy – is it fair, just or hypocritical to destroy his efforts at creating a family?"

"He's a monster," Amber says.

"But I have to learn to love that monster," Hanna says, and takes a deep breath.

Ahead in the dark are the Guardians and Reese waving flashlights, signaling for the coven to come closer.

"We know where he is," Reese says.

"In the catacombs beneath the mountain," Gladys says.

"But the Goddess has flooded the catacombs," Hanna exhales.

"Not here. Not this mountain."

"The demon keeps to his lair – in the cavernous hollows."

"Clairvoyance is strong here," Reese says, "I can see and feel their presence. Leisha tends to the baby when the witch, if that's what she should be called, is out casting her magic."

Out of the brush comes Thor stopping to lick his wounds.

"And now you know how we found the catacombs," Reese says.

"What happened?" Hanna questions.

"You've been star gazing," Vienna steps in.

"I cannot deny my connection to sorcery now that I have found my maternal grandmother – I have learned from my elder."

"Well, we've lost the army and the following but we still have the Shamans," Amber says.

"But the army battles the shadows – we believe that is why there is still peace here," Sydney says.

"Perhaps the demon does not know where we are, or that we are here," Paisley says.

"Nonsense, sister," Priscilla says, "the demon has his own witch. And those birds – a flock of totems with a watchful eye … someone should be sensing us – as close as we are."

"It depends," Vienna insists, "if star gazing has thrown her off track – they may not know how close we got to her."

"How close?" Hanna exhales.

"We could hear her – she's tended by Leisha – she is a Guardian, and like us, she can sense and feel the connection that the Guardians share."

"Then they do know we are close."

"Not if she sensed your body double or some magic involved – remote viewing can be done from any point."

"Did you go as you are now?"

"Yes, we did. Thor lead us there but we got stopped short of getting to her and had to retreat, then we heard a scuffle with Thor – likely the witch has a totem as guard."

"What stopped you?

"The smell of death," Vienna drops her head. "We felt that the demon must be among the shadows – the demon wreaks of death and the shadows bring on the cold."

"So much for Hell's inferno," Amber says.

"When Hell freezes over," Priscilla says.

"That's when we find her," Hanna says adamantly.

From the forest edge, following Thor's tracks are Eva, Herman, and Drake running urgently with the cries of a baby in tow.

"Aly!" Hanna screams.

"Run!" Herman says with a steady voice.

She runs toward them and falls to her knees.

"Aly!" She exclaims.

"The witch is dead," Herman yells.

"There were no Guardians," Eva says panting, faint of breath.

"Just the witch," Drake says, "but she is dead... no one here killed her, but she had a blade through her chest... her blood all over Thor... and then he was attacked... bitten by the demon, don't know if he'll live." Drake breathes.

"You better run," Herman says, grabbing onto Hanna with a fist; before them stands Jace, his face alert with eyes protruding like the demon; he smiles faintly with fanged teeth like a great wolf – then, a thunder rolls from his voice, a loud dissonant hum, with the force of an avalanche behind him; the mountain is a rolling thunder.

"Jace!" Hanna screams, "You have lost your way," and behind him is Lucius who bends on one knee, "I am promised to the night my love," he says and the two of them vanish into the dark fog as the avalanche rolls toward them.

"Run!" Herman exhales and as quick as lightning a flash appears in the horizon and the mountain begins to crumble...

"It's Maine again!" Sydney yells and they have no time to summons the Goddess, and Jace, again, with a closed fist pounds his cold flesh to the earth which splits, breaking apart in two jutted peaks, and Thor yelps, taking leave on an injured paw until Drake tosses the bruised dog over his shoulder and they run and keep running with the landscape closing in on them; they are thrust forward into a spiraling portal that takes them to the cold abyss. The land is dismal; the immensity of the avalanche crushed the lodging of Connecticut but they have somehow found themselves in between like a state of limbo where there is no light – no solar energy – no celestial light and they learn that the entire town's folks are among them – absorbed by the dark abyss of space where they float lightly as if in a dream.

Hanna, after locating a flare, lights the abyss - a place of time and space unlike the inner realm – an outer realm like a void – finally she gets her hands on her daughter for the first time. Side-by-side the siblings unite cradled in their mother's chest and they touch one another for the first time; she cradles them there…

"I don't know how I know but I know that Jace has placed us here," Hanna says, "Both of them have given themselves to the night – they have sworn themselves to the monster so their children will have a place to live."

"The Prophecy," Sydney says, floating freely among the dark spaces "do you have it?"

Hanna wears her gear: knapsack, Gore Tex coat and cargo pants. Within her gear she carries the athame blade, the rose quartz chalice, the books of Prophecy Volumes I and II, sticks of flares and upon her neck she wears both amulets given to her by Sydney and Reese.

She weeps seeing her daughter's face, who has grown over one year.

"What does the book say to do?" Sydney interrupts and Hanna removes the book from her knapsack and hands it over to Sydney. She quickly examines the book, "We are stuck in limbo," she says, "we have a critical choice to make for our next move to be right."

As Alysiah and Lucas Daniel's wrist meet the power of the sacred emerge from the darkness; Helga, with golden wings of the Phoenix and the Prince of Peace with an angelic face presides among them, "As above, so below," Helga says and her eyes flash with red, "we shall restore harmony," she says when a light like a distant tunnel illuminates among them.

"There shall be peace," Sydney says, and the Celestial beings retreat – but Hanna can see the spark of light in her children's eyes and she begins to follow the trail of light that takes them to the outer realm where Grandall stands regal with a staff as tall as his body and Sterling shimmers aside Tully in Celestial Light. Then, with a force of one thousand horses the light begins to break and the darkness enters the light where all becomes gray.

"The dark has found the light," Sydney says.

"And the light has found the dark," Grandall says, waving his staff where a portal opens and the Shamans gather around them, "it is time," he says, feeling the energy of Celestial Light diminish in the density of dark matter among them.

And Hanna holds tightly.

"Star gazing may serve you well," he says to Hanna, "but now is the time that the powers will be equal in number and strength – but only one can succeed and restore the New Order."

"What is the New Order? How do we follow what we do not know?"

"The order is within you."

"Brace yourselves," Herman says, "the dark is upon us, and the shadows of the night find the light – bringing in the frost from the cold."

The sound of jarring screaming casts upon them and Grandall raises his staff in the eyes of terror – the demon with a shrilling voice before him.

He guffaws a shrieking howl, standing erect on hind legs, and Grandall blocks one swift swoop with the sacred staff when the two women levitate before them – "Give to us the child," Goldie spats with a pointed index finger.

"Give us what we desire and he shall no longer suffer," Leisha says, with Lucius hung from his feet and the Ravens begin to ravish his body.

"I am the light," he says, in a faraway voice – his ethereal body illuminated in the dark. "What you have is empty." He spats back and the demon takes possession of his body and in his wrath he tosses him to the side - a mangled victim.

"As you will find their fathers," the demon says when Jace emerges, hanging lopsided by the foot when he dissipates in thin air – disappearing into the dense, and fog-like atmosphere.

"Where is he?" The demon beckons and flares his bat-like wings – and with a claw across her face, he aims to seize her there with both an infant and a child cradled to her chest, and she falls, clutching each one, sure to never let them go, and reaches for the athame blade – her hand to the cold metal.

Candace Meredith

Twenty-Six

The physical realm crumbles all around them. The dark blankets the light like a fog over the stars. The Druid's Army has seized the vacant ship and set fire to it unaware that the demon exists in a dual in the outer realm where only a portal can take them.

Archibald leads his army to the water's edge where the avalanche did not reach but the Shamans' homes are once again destroyed. Luther, along with the Warlock's Coven, follow the army's lead and Bernard finds them just in time for another try to seize the demon before he makes himself immortal by the blood of the Divine Ones. The Quakers of Maine follow suit to defeat the shadows before any more destruction can commence.

"Much of New England lives in peril," Bernard says looking at the snow before them.

"All of New England is shrouded in darkness," Luther says.

The Shamans following the wisdom of the animals have moved to higher ground where the avalanche did not touch. The Ravens leave their perch on the branches of skinny trees. Connecticut is in ruin among fire and snowfall; the army and all of the following who have been salvaged await pending sacrament between good and evil. There is a sensing and a knowing among Pagans and Wiccans who sense and feel the adversity of one another's demise. And, although the book is blank – they have an inner knowing that they are following Divine faith.

"As above, so below," Hanna repeats, "that must mean the covens – the army – must be back."

And as Hanna speaks the fortress beneath them gives way and they find themselves tumbling like a whirlwind in a vortex to the ground below; Hanna lands in the water, melted by fire, carrying her two young children.

"Get her out of the water," Luther exhales.

"She has another child upon her chest," Goldie exclaims, "we must seize both!"

"There will never be a Beltane – there will never be a ceremony – you have met your end," Sydney says, bracing herself as Goldie extends her forefinger and Sydney's body is sent flying across the ice and into the fire, then, Archibald throws himself into the embers to bring out her body.

"I am going to feed you as carrion to the birds," the demon growls and Sydney rubs her fingers over her amulet and the massive cat lurches, swiping its large paws when the demon sinks its fangs into the scruff of the neck sending Thor from the flames and onto its back; the demon lurches sending both animals into the water.

"Where are the Elders?" Amber screams.

"The light has no duty on Earth," Leisha spats and makes a run for it – toward Hanna – toward the blessed siblings, but the army fights hard blocking her path when the Ravens land upon them and begin scratching and pecking at their faces and their bare necks.

"Use the athame," Hanna hears from far away as Goldie snaps her fingers appearing in two places at once and snatches the cradled infant from her grasp and knocks Hanna off her feet with the slice of her hand and tosses the child into the air – the baby screaming. She is caught by the reach of the demon.

"Now the other one," he says, "Hurry," and holds the child with her bare skin to the cold air.

"Shed your blood," Lucius' voice says from far away again, like a distant bell.

Leisha grabs her blade from its scabbard and pierces the flesh of the Druid's Army follower, cutting her way to the water's edge when she disappears, re-appearing behind Hanna, grabbing onto her hair – she lets out a howling scream.

"Follow your intuition," she hears Sterling's voice from the cosmos as Lucas Daniel is stolen from her body.

"Now bring him to me," the demon breathes and the temperature of the inner realm drops below freezing and their breath creates a dewy frost as they speak. Hanna shakes nervously with her hands trembling; she takes the athame blade, drops to her knees, out of Leisha's clutch.

"Stop her!" Goldie exhales and Hanna slices her left hand, pouring her blood into the chalice and the demon takes his first taste of her child's blood at the wrist bearing the crescent birthmark and transforms into the gaunt face of a man making him half immortal when the Goddess of Celestial Light leaves her body and is trapped there by the dark shadows –

"Now!" Jace bellows from behind the demon holding a blade and Hanna instinctively removes the chalice, plunges the athame blade into it and bellows his name: "Herschel Lambert Beecham!"

"Say it again," Sydney yells.

"The power of three!" Vienna hollers.

"Hurry," Gladys says.

"No! You fools," Goldie says, throwing Vienna off her feet with kinetic energy induced by a crooked wand.

"Your telekinesis cannot save her," she says and is jolted by Goldie again.

Then, Gladys steps in, picking Vienna off the ground when Luther lunges upon Leisha, holding her to the ground.

"Say it with love in your heart," Grandall says as the mountain crumbles around them and Luther takes his grandson into his arms.

"I have love in my heart," she beckons aloud as the demon takes Aly's neck into his grasp, leaning in for the fatal bite to send immortality into himself and the child who shall become his heir over the darkness – Hanna slams the athame blade into the bowl of the chalice and Jace, with the face of fire, drives a sword blade through the demon's spine, causing him to drop Aly, losing her from his clutch, and is caught by Goldie who holds her tight — and yields a blade in her palm.

"You cannot have her back," she glowers with piercing eyes.

"There is no love like that of a father for his daughter," Jace screams.

"Or the love of a father for his son," Luther says.

"Or a mother for her child," Goldie sneers.

"Or the love of a friend," Hanna says.

"You have to do it once more," Jace says and Hanna unscrews the cap of the athame blade handle and pours the rose water into the chalice and she submerges the blade, "Herschel Lambert Beecham!" She exhales, "you are not alone."

Then, emanating from her daughter, glowing brighter, surrounded by dark shadows is the Goddess of Celestial light and from her son emerges the Prince of Peace with Jace standing among them; he hands his daughter over to her mother as Goldie folds under his immense power, "Atlas, the Prince of Peace," he yells, "you no longer represent sorrow or fear," he continues, removing the sword from the demon's back who has morphed to full mortal form, and lays upon the ground as Mr. Beecham, breathing mildly with his scarred face to the wind – "You now, as ever, represent empathy and virtue. I am now the ruler of the underworld – and am the representation of sorrow, fear, and angst that is among you!"

"Jace, no," Hanna says.

"Then as ruler of the underworld you shall show mercy," the Goddess, in an image of a golden phoenix, says.

"Yes," Jace says, "beginning with the life I took – a life taken, can be given back," and so he points his hands up above, bringing down the mangled body, "Elder of the Light I summons you," he says, laying the remnants of Lucius' body upon the ground.

Grandall, the Celestial Elder, appears among them and he does not speak, instead, he raises his staff, hovering over the body and a spark of Celestial Light glimmers from the rubbish, then, engulfs the body, flooding him with light, repairing his damaged bones and skin. Lucius quivers on the ground momentarily.

"No one dies in a Holy War," Jace says, facing Sydney, "they just transform."

"And to what transformation have you taken?" Grandall questions.

"The ruler of the dark – the ruler who shall show mercy on those who do harm – to find in them the good - to transform the darkness to greatness."

With that message, Grandall raises his staff over the shadows who transform back to the men and the women they once were.

"And for the Shaman you killed?" Grandall says.

"The only permanent death is one done by a demon. There is mercy in what appears to be cruel."

Then Grandall smiles, and from the portal emerges the Shaman. Grandall then turns to Mr. Beecham who tries to stand to his feet holding his aching back when Grandall moves his staff to the point of entrance, using the light to heal his wound.

Thor limps with pain to stand aside Jace, licking his hand and whimpering slightly.

Jace pats his smooth fur and nudges his head. And Grandall turns to Goldie, "She is not yours I presume."

Goldie stutters morosely, "Let up my cousin and we shall leave them to you."

"Promise?" Grandall smiles humbly, "then we shall let you go."

Goldie races to her, demanding that Luther let her go. Leisha gets to her feet as Luther removes his boots from her throat and the two of them flee.

"You could hardly care about me now," Mr. Beecham says, "all you wanted was power," he cries, and Goldie stares back looking candid.

"You are weak and frail," she hisses through the dark, "now open me a portal," she says frankly.

"I'm afraid you're going to have to walk where you are going," Grandall says.

"I'm afraid the darkness has hindered that energy field for you now," Sydney chides.

"Fine," she says, standing her distance, and drags her slacks through the mud.

Hanna takes her son and her daughter in her arms once more, and Lucius wraps his arms around the three of them. "He did it for us," he says.

"I know," she whispers.

"There is a great deal of repairing to do," Grandall explains, then he touches his staff to the ground creating a stream-like crack in the earth's surface, opening the ground to allow the light to shine through, and as the darkness dissipates a new order emerges – a great city rises from the earth's core, erupting in pristine mountains capped with snow.

"I can give to all of you a piece of Celestial magic – a new order in which to live."

"It's like Shambhala on earth," Paisley says.

"Yes, it is sister," Sydney says, "Yes, it is."

Luther approaches his son, "I knew you would be back," he says, patting his hand to his shoulder.

"And I always knew you'd be back for me," Lucius smiles.

"Now we can go home," Helga says, waving her wings – "you always had the courage inside of you but I was the light you needed in order to find it."

"The energies are in harmony," the Prince of Peace says, and with the wave of his hand a motion of white light spirals like a funnel until he and Helga vanish from the physical plane.

"I am also not of this dimension," Grandall says, and with the wave of his staff he departs, too.

Jace gives another pat behind Thor's ear, "You are to stay here in the realm of my daughter," he says waving him off and Thor follows suit, wincing momentarily then Jace transforms into the body of the phantom, with the toss of his hand he waves them off and disappears like water vapor.

The Covens, the army, the followers and the Shamans learn a new order in the great mountains.

And Hanna's body awakens.

But somewhere hissing from the deep is an old woman who breathes, "You haven't killed this old crone," she croaks and from the depths of the expansive darkness she lurks. Contemplating.

Epilogue

On the Eve of the Summer Solstice the pagans celebrate the longest day with a midsummer ceremony; in the great city spanning over Vermont and Connecticut the community of Shamans and Pagans gather in a ritual among the great circle to thank the Goddess, the Elders, the Prince and each other. The underworld is still cold and cavernous; the people there find solace in healing their anger, fear and sorrow in practices that only Pagans, Wiccans and Shamans share; by drawing down the moon and summonsing the Goddess who spreads her wings of the Phoenix over them – and they rise from their own ashes – to suffer no more.

Herschel Beecham finds solace alongside Thor – an attentive hunting dog that aids him in bringing feasts to the people of the ski resort. Leisha and Goldie hide themselves in the gauntlet of narrow peaks where they await a return of a master of the dark. Sterling and Tully reside above as Elders of the Celestial Vision and the Druids' Army live among the Shamans who practice sorcery and magic to bring peace and prosperity to the people of the new order: compassion.

About the Author

Candace Meredith earned her Bachelor of Science degree in English Creative Writing from Frostburg State University in the spring of 2008. Her works of poetry, photography and fiction have appeared in literary journals Bittersweet, Backbone Mountain Review, Anthology 17, Greensilk Journal, Saltfront and The Broadkill Review. She currently works as a Freelance Editor for an online publishing company and has earned her Master of Science degree in Integrated Marketing and Communications (IMC) from West Virginia University.

Visit Candace's Author Page At:

www.ctupublishinggroup.com/candace-meredith.html

Made in the USA
Middletown, DE
31 January 2020